**SYREN RAVENWOOD**

# THE DEVIL HEAD
## Rivals From Collided Paths

**BLUEROSE PUBLISHERS**
India | U.K.

Copyright © Syren Ravenwood 2025

All rights reserved by author. No part of this publication may be reproduced, stored in a retrieval system or transmitted in any form or by any means, electronic, mechanical, photocopying, recording or otherwise, without the prior permission of the author. Although every precaution has been taken to verify the accuracy of the information contained herein, the publisher assumes no responsibility for any errors or omissions. No liability is assumed for damages that may result from the use of information contained within.

BlueRose Publishers takes no responsibility for any damages, losses, or liabilities that may arise from the use or misuse of the information, products, or services provided in this publication.

For permissions requests or inquiries regarding this publication, please contact:

**BLUEROSE PUBLISHERS**
www.BlueRoseONE.com
info@bluerosepublishers.com
+91 8882 898 898
+4407342408967

ISBN: 978-93-7018-458-9

Cover design: Daksh
Typesetting: Tanya Raj Upadhyay

First Edition: April 2025

# The Devil Head Playlist

Call out my name - *The Weekend*
Black Sea. - *Natasha Blume*
I'm yours. - *Oryl*
Streets (silhouette remix) - *Doja Cat*
Frozen. - *Circle Bob*
Love is a b\*\*\*\*. - *Two feets*
Go f\*\*\* yourself - *Two feets*
Look at me now - *Brennan Savage*
Bad Karma - *Alex Thesleff*
Baby doll - *Ari Abdul*
Roses - *Saint JHN*
Desire. (Hucci remix) - *Meg Myres*
Dangerous. - *Jake Warren*
All I want. - *Sarah Blasko*
Angel. - *Camylio demo*
Living life in the night. - *Cheriimoya, Sierra kidd.*
Breathe in, breathe out. - *David Kushsner*
Outta the blue. - *Nicolas Bonnin*
Whoopty (ers remix). - *CJ*
Jinaa (original mix). - *Bö & Defox*
Clandestina (JVSTIN remix). - *Filv & Edmofo feat. Emma peters.*

Boom - *Ibenji feat. Talabun*
I can't do this. - *K3NT4*
Ecstasy. - *Suicidal Idol*
Red sex. - *Vessel*
New jeans (Jersey remix) - *Jiandro x Dxrkaii*
00:00. - *LAGXNA*
Possession - *Cheyanne*
Drowning. - *Vague003*
Pop like this pt.2. - *CPK Shawn*
Life force. - *RJ pasin*
Lobster. - *RJ pasin*
Oh yeah. - *Yello*
Genesis. - *Bravo 1-2.*
Beautiful life (mike key remix). - *Xassa*
Montagem Coral. - *Dj Holanda*
Xtayalive. - *JNHYGS*
Demons in my soul - *SCXR Soul xSxInxwy*
Angel by wings - *MTG Da Sia*
Poussiere d'empire. - *Nessbeal (feat. Indila)*
Robot Rock (funk)super slowed - *Dj paulinho Mondi Da Baixa Baviera*
**Минимум (Ramzan Abitov remix)** - *ямаджи*
**Фонтанчик с дельФином (adam maniac & Iman bek remix)** - *гио пика*

Spotify like of the devil Head playlist:
https://open.spotify.com/playlist/7uQSHvWzcNve3dIjYZoPyS?si=S8ZQd1NhRVC-ob7pq2Cs2w&pi=3y5rsJoRR5avs

*Warning*

A Note of Caution from the Author, Syren Ravenwood:

Dear Readers,
Before you delve into the dark world of "The Devil Head," I feel it's crucial to offer a sincere word of caution. This story explores intense themes of violence, brutality, moral ambiguity, organized crime, smuggling, strong language, revenge, retribution, mafia wars, kidnapping, torture, graphic violence, bloodshed, psychological manipulation and dark themes of obsession and romance. Reader discretion is advised. The characters navigate a world of crime, where ruthless actions and decisions are often portrayed.

It is imperative to understand that the actions depicted in this story are not intended to be glorified, romanticized, or emulated. These are extreme scenarios within a fictional context. I urge readers to maintain a clear distinction between fantasy and reality.

Furthermore, "The Devil Head" contains scenes and descriptions that may be disturbing to some. While not explicitly detailed, the story also touches upon the potential for mental health struggles within the characters, given their violent lifestyles and traumatic experiences.

Reader prudence is strongly advised. Thank you for respecting my wishes regarding the distribution of this work. Your understanding is greatly appreciated.

Sincerely,

Syren Ravenwood

# THE
DEVIL HEAD

The Devil Head, the name of the story, is associated with its script. Here, it refers to a person who lets the inner devil take control. I.e. the person loses his temper and starts punishing, torturing and killing his rivals in a most brutal way that the appropriate word of that will be the devil's way. So, the person is also having the mindset of a devil, that's what, this book name is " *THE DEVIL HEAD*"

*Destruction*

*Entrenched*

*Vengeance*

*Illicit*

*Lords*

*To those who crave the edge of the seat, and are unafraid to witness its brutal art. May this story be dangerously sweet, and leave you forever changed by its sin.*

# PART 1

## -The Shattered City-

I, I...am Adira (Stammering) And I am laying between the tall buildings of Moscow, while my husband is burning the city. I have no idea, from where, which part of which building would fall over me and crush my injured body. With a broken and fully injured body, but a satisfied soul, all I was thinking right now was the best memories of my life. But I was still filled with some Questions. Why was my whole life, I was called a monster under the human skin ? Why hasn't my husband ever known with these kinds of names ? aren't the people aware the side of his, I saw today ? If they would've they would never let him rise. And the biggest question was, Was i really deserve it ? Was I really a monster ? Why was I blamed my whole life, for being a monster and not the people who made me a monster ? Is it really the end of my life ? But then.....

*Blood lust awakens, darkness descends,*
*Slay the rival, claims the amend.*
*In shadow cast, where steel meets bone*
*Victory's sweet in the enemy's throne.*
*In this game of power & might*
*Slay or be slain, in endless nights.*
*Cut the throat of mercy's plea,*
*bathe in blood, wild & free.*
*Rise oh, lord, with heart of night,*
*Dance with death, in immortal fights.*

*Rostov-on-Don,* a city carved into the underbelly of Russia, had long worn a grim reputation. Its name conjured images of shadowy figures, back alley deals, and the brutal calculus of organized crime. Smuggling routes snaked through its ports, human lives were traded like commodities in its hidden corners, and the echoes of violence often stained its dark, polluted streets. The very air seemed to hum with a low frequency of menace, a constant thrum of danger that vibrated up from the cobblestones. The city's nights, in particular, were a symphony of screams – some of pain, some of rage, some of desperation – a stark testament to the lawlessness that held sway.

But now, an unsettling quiet had descended. Rostov-on-Don was living in **Trattativa**– (a negotiated peace), a truce struck between the warring factions that had long battled for control. This wasn't a peace born of morality or a sudden collective enlightenment. It was a ceasefire forged in necessity, hammered out in clandestine meetings where the scent of blood and the promise of profit mingled in the air. The silence that now blanketed the city was not the silence of tranquility, but the silence of a coiled serpent, a predator holding its breath.

The absence of overt violence was palpable. The nightly screams had faded, replaced by an eerie stillness that felt almost more ominous. The streets, once slick with rain and shadowed by the threat of ambush, now seemed merely...empty. The usual tension hadn't vanished; it had simply gone underground, simmering beneath the surface like a subterranean fire.

Enforcers still patrolled, but their movements were less brazen, their weapons less openly displayed. Deals were still struck, but with a newfound caution, a wary eye cast over the shoulder. The city held its breath, waiting, anticipating the inevitable moment when the Trattativa would crumble, and the old ways would return with renewed ferocity. For in Rostov-on-Don, peace was often just another form of war, fought in whispers and shadows, and measured not in bodies but in the shifting balance of power."

**I am Adira,** I was called a rare combination of beauty & brain. My 5'10 feet height used to enhance my aura, making it more powerful and strong. My piercing silver eyes, like a winter storm, seemed to freeze time, commanding attention without a word. My fair complexion , smooth as alabaster, belied the steel forged within. My Raven-black hair cascaded down my back, framing the face that was both beautiful and terrifying. My calm demeanor, a carefully crafted facade. My gaze absorbs every detail. I wasn't so fond of violence. But still, I was the most feared and revered figure in the underworld. My piercing silver gaze, sliced through their shadows, striking fear into the hearts of even the most hardened criminals. My soft, confident voice was laced with an unspoken threat that froze blood in veins. My warth leaves only ashes in its wake. Souls who dares cross my path are never seen again. Some people used to call me "*The La Regina della*" which means '*queen of death*'. People used to call me this because I had no weakness or.....they were not aware of it.

Yes, this 'La Regina della', also had a weakness. Someone I would burn the world for. Someone I would never hesitate to lay dead bodies for. Becoming a gangster was never my choice but my situations for raising up this person and up making me a gangster.

**Krish,** my younger brother, the only weakness, my world used to revolve around him. I was his everything, mother, sister, teacher, guardian and everything. His life was not similar to the other people of his age. Of course he was the brother of Russia's one of the most reputed and terrifying Mafia. He never went to college for safety reasons. He was not allowed to go outside without the security.

---

# CHAPTER 1

## The La Regina Della

*"Happy birthday to you !","Happy birthday to you !"* the crowd cheering *'thunderous applause'*. *"Happy Birthday Krish"*, I cheered. *"Thank you so much, Di "(Di-elder sister)* Krish replied. *"I love you so much."* I gushed and pressed a kiss to his forehead. Everybody was celebrating his birthday when suddenly my phone buzzed loudly.*"Excuse me, I need to receive this one."* I excused myself. It was a call from *Zara, ( the fourth narrator) She was also* known as *Zaharia Azeena, <u>is a striking woman with a presence that commands attention. She stands tall at 5'8", a height that contributes to her confident demeanor. Her complexion is fair, smooth as alabaster, a contrast to the often dark and dangerous world she navigates.</u>*

<u>*Her most defining characteristic is her serious demeanor. Zara is not one for frivolousness; her expressions are usually measured and thoughtful. This seriousness reflects her role as my underboss and her unwavering loyalty. She is a "loyalist faith keeper with an unchanging personality," a woman upon whom I can always rely.*</u>

"*Zara, where are you ? I'm so goddamn furious that you are late.*" I fumed but paused when I didn't hear any response. "*Hello ? Zara ?*" I mused.

Suddenly the sound of a gunshot echoed through the phone, accompanied by a terrified wail, To listen to it carefully. I asked to stop the music, but no one listened, I repeated it, and still the music was on. *"Turn off the fucking Dj."* I roared in frustration. A sudden echoing silence followed my outburst. I was panting heavily after my outburst. Then placed the phone back against my ear, listening attentively to the sound to my tempest rooted as I heard the sound. My eyes widened and I gripped the phone tightly as I realized what was going on. Suddenly the call dropped. Everybody. stood there in silence. Then suddenly, my phone rang again and I quickly picked it up. *"Adira"* Zara cried out *"We've been. Attacked" I shrieked. "The Nova Spire is in danger now"*

(Nova spire is the hub of my gang, which takes care of the assets, properties and internal, external affair of our gang. It is the coordination point.) Zara begged *"Adira, order eves to attack back."* ( *eves* - gang members of my gang. It is the short form of evils)

*"Take the offensive,"* I ordered in a dead tone. Then the call disconnected. I paused there. And a tense expression was visible on my face. Then I suddenly

looked around and put a facade on my face. I walked toward the stage and climbed on it. I raised both my hands and clapped in the air, trying to get everyone's attention and distract them from what had happened just now.

*"I command your attention"* I spoke authoritatively, my words carrying weight and confidence. Everybody turned to me. *"I'm so glad that you gave your precious time and blessings to the piece of my heart, Krish. Thank you so much for attending this function and making it more joyful for us with your great enthusiasm. And Krish..... Happy 18th birthday. You know I love you."* I said with no expression on my face with attitude and confidence in my words. *"I wish I had more time with you, guys. But wishes really come true. Now, I have to leave. You guys can enjoy the party."* And then I smiled for less than a second and came down from the stage and left. Krish tried to stop me, but I ignored him. On my way to the **Nova spire** I was just thinking about how my gang members' condition would be when i will reach there. Who are the attackers? And all, I was drowning in these thoughts. I wanted to get there as soon as possible. As I reached, I rushed out of the car and

rushed inside the Nova Spire. Everything was over. Every Eve including Zara was sitting in the conference room. I skidded to a stop when I saw Zara and others. I took a breath of reprieve . A sense of calmness washed over me. Zara stood up as she saw me. I ran to Zara and hugged her so tight. Everybody there had injuries. After hugging her, I stepped back. *"Who stopped you to attack back? I never asked you to seek my permission, did I ?"* I questioned.

*"No, you never did."* Zara solanced. *"But we had to ask you, cause the attackers were..."* Zara hesitated.

*"Were ?"* I raised my eyebrows and asked.

*"They were the Raos."* Zara gasped. ( **Raos, are the gang members of another mafia** )

*"Anyone left to be killed ?"* I hissed

"No." Zara replied.

*"So, first tell me what had happened"* I asked.

*"Raos came to capture our Nova Spire, and you know once they have our Nova Spire, they will have our assets, properties and all. But being a mafia, they were not supposed to attack on the mafia, who was included in the*

*agreement of 1927...But I think,we should not take this as a serious matter cause it's their job."*

*"Then it's our job to protect our Nova Spire."* I bursted. Everyone in the hall went silent for a few minutes. Then Zara broke the silence and asked in a tense tone, *"Did we just invite a new rival?"* I looked at Zara, and after some seconds, I said *"No, they did."* Everybody again went silent.

*"Who's their leader?"* i asked

*"Lennox Desmond D'arcy."* Zara replied.

*"Oh. the great Russian physico."* I confirmed.

# LENNOX DESMOND D'ARCY, leader of the raos.

He was known as the "Great Russian Physico" or "The gay mafia." Though, he was the leader but still he wasn't straight. He was a foolish man, weird to think, he was the most idiotic person with no limits of stupidity. This self-proclaimed mafia kingpin was known for his bloated ego, garish suit and staggering stupidity. His 'brilliant' plans often ended in comedic chaos, earning eye rolls from loyal- yet exasperated - henchmen. Lennox's narcissism was only rivaled by his psychosis paranoid episodes fueled by cocaine and his own inflated sense of importance. Though he was a foolish man, he was still so good at enmity. He would experiment on his rivals, find more joyful, and hazard ways to kill a man. And that was the only thing that would make people afraid of him. Moreover, he had one of the biggest army of his people among the top 10 underworlds of Russia. wWith high level weapons.

**1927,** a contract of negotiated peace was signed by almost every underworld is Russia. This contract was between the government of Russia and the Russian mafias. The contract was that the underworlds will never hurt or interfere between any internal or external affair of any citizen of Russia. And they will never destroy any public property. And the Russian government will never interfere between the external or internal affairs of any mafia, unless they have not violated any rule of Russia.

With this, there was another contract between the underworlds. The underworlds had divided the areas. And any underworld cannot get into any area without the permission of the underworld who owns that area.

# PRESENT TIME

I suddenly got an unknown call on my phone. A few seconds later, I picked it up. It took me a few seconds to realise that it was Lennox on the other side of the call. He said, " *I'm so sorry, Adira. It was all my fault. I didn't know that you owned the Nove Spire. You know, it's so famous, it just lured me. I've made a mistake. I'm sorry....*"

*"I'm glad you realised."*

*" I hope nobody has died."*

*" They are just injured."*

*"Thank god. But...my people haven't arrived yet. I think you might have killed 'em."*

*"Aaa...actually I did. But don't expect an apology from me."*

*"Nah, it's okay. They were really useless, if they got killed ... .But I'm not done apologizing yet. Listen, Adira, Tomorrow it's my birthday, and I asked Raos for Nova Spire, as my birthday gift. But now, as I cannot have Nova Spire, can I?"*

*"Not a chance."*

*" Yeah, so I want you...you to present at my birthday party. It's a humble request. Either it will be a battle or a new relationship. I would go for a new relationship."*

*"If you don't want a battle, then why would I ?"*

*"Wow. I expect you to see you at the party tomorrow at 7:30 in the evening, at my mansion."*

After I hung up the call. I stood still in surprise. I just wasn't expecting this.

Zara was feeling the same. *"What the heck"*

*"Is it supposed to be good news or bad?"* Zara asked and continued, *"Well, ask my suggestion. You should not go there."*

.*"I know. But I heard him on the phone. And I'm done making new rivals "* I said.

*"Nevertheless, I'm against it. And still if you wanna go. Then, don't go alone."* Zara replied.

*" Of course. You'll come."* I said.

*"Okay, you go alone."* Zara replied.

After the conversation ended, I left for my home. As I reached back home, I was caught up by Krish. I continued walking while Krish was following me.

"*What happened?*" Krish asked with a tensed face

"*Why are you awake till late ?*"

"*That's not the point.*"

"*Oh. That is the point.*"

"*Di, why do you think I'm a goddamn child?*"

"*Cause, you are.*"

"*I know you're mafia, what to hide now?*" I stopped and looked at my wrist watch, and said, "*It's 1:30 am. Now, your birthday is gone. Now, don't you ever think that I cannot slap you.*"

"*Yes, you can. You have the rights. But do I have the right to know what's going on in my sister's life?*"

I paused and looked deep into Krish's eyes and said, "No."

Krish gasped and went back to his room.

The hours bled into one another, a restless tide carrying me closer to the party. A part of me dreaded it, the forced smiles and the suffocating pretense, but another part, a darker, more impulsive part, craved the distraction. Zara, bless her stubborn heart, had practically taken up residence in our home, her presence a constant, reassuring anchor. It meant Krish wasn't alone, not truly, and that eased the gnawing anxiety that always seemed to claw at my throat these days.

As the time drew near, I finished the last touches of my preparation, the silk of my dress whispering against my skin like a secret. Before I slipped out the door, I found myself drawn to Krish's room. I sat next to him, on his bed. Krish was still angry with me. I could feel it in the way he avoided my gaze, the clipped tone of his voice whenever he was forced to address me, the almost imperceptible stiffening of his shoulders when I came too close. It was a cold, simmering anger, unlike the fiery outbursts I was more accustomed to from him. This was a silent withdrawal, a shutting down, and in some ways, it was far more unsettling.

"Still angry ?" I asked politely.

*"Yeah. any doubt ?"*

"Hey, look at me." Krish ignored me.

*"Krish, look at me. You're clearly aware that if you stop talking to me, I feel lifeless. You know what are the worst days of my life ? when I spend the days without looking at you, talking to you. The best part of the day is waking you up in the morning. Feeding you, and might be scolding you too."*

Krish chuckled. And I continued," *I never want you to be tense, that's why I never tell you anything.*"

"*Di, I promise, I won't think about it much. Now please tell me.*" Krish requested.

"Someone had attacked Nova Spire. But now it's all sorted."

"*So simple it was.*"

Then I gushed a kiss on his forehead and got up and said,"*don't be awake till late.*" *as i was about to leave,* Krish asked " *when will you be back ?*" I paused and looked at him and sighed. "*So soon.*"

And I left. For the party. I soon reached the venue.

I am Rauf Miroslava ( the second narrator of the story ) . I was an uncle of one of the great Russian mafia. I Was also invited with that mafia to Lennox's birthday party. I first saw Adira at Lennox's birthday Party.

I still remember, as she entered a vision darkness & sophistication emerged, commanding the attention of every guest in the opulent ballroom. Her raven- black hair cascaded down her back like a waterfall of nights perfectly complementing the sleek, black mermaid dress that hugged her curves like a second skin.

The dress was a masterpiece of design, with intricate silver embroidery that seemed to shimmer and dance in the light, like the stars on a clear, moonless night.

As she glided across the room, her confident stride eating up the distance, the air seemed to vibrate with an almost palpable sense of anticipation. Who was this enigmatic woman and what secrets lay hidden behind those piercing, silver eyes?

And then, with a subtle smile, she began to move, her body weaving through the crowd with a fluid predatory grace, lasting a trail of intrigue and speculation in her wake.

As Lennox saw Adira, he went to her hurriedly and welcomed her warm heartedly.

*"Adira, The La Regina Della. You don't even need to use weapons to kill a person, your looks are enough."*

*"Nice to meet you in person, Lennox. And happy birthday."*

*"Thanks."*

*"Here's a small gift for you."*

*"OMG! Graff Diamonds Hallucination ? Are you fucking kidding me, girl ? This is the most precious gift ever. I wanna*

cry. Thank you so much, Adira. Love you. I'm o'er the moon."

"It's all my pleasure."

"And I forgot to give you a surprise."

"Surprise? for me?"

"Not for you. For our new relationship. Please don't say no."

"Okay, so, where's my surprise?"

"Waiting for you."

"Huh ?"

"Waiting for you."

"At home?" Her eyes narrowed

"Yes. Oh, wait. Are you, are you doubting? on me?"

" I mean no. I'm not doubting you."

"So, can I expect you to stay long?"

"Ahmm. Actually I would have to leave soon."

Now, I was clearly able to see tension on her face, maybe it was because of Lennox's statement, so it was easy to understand that she wanted to leave as soon as possible.

In the crowd of the people who were staring at Adira. There was someone, who was admiring her. Thinking she was the best creation of god. He was so drowned in her eyes that he even forgot to breathe. He forced himself to look away, but he just couldn't. Then I noticed him, and helped him by getting his sudden attention.

*"She's Adira."*

*"No, I was just..."* Then I interrupted again. *" Rivaan. She's the La Regina Della, your obsession."*

*"No way."*

*"What happened ?"*

*"When I looked at her, it gave me an idea that The La Regina Della must look like her."*

*"Well she's The La Regina Della herself."*

**RIVAAN,** also known by his alias Riaan. He was one of the biggest mafia of Russia. A formidable and enigmatic figure in the world of organised crime His piercing golden eyes seem to bore into those he meets. Rivaan's chiseled features, his 6 '6 feet height and strong, sharp jawline are accentuated by his sharp, tailored suits, which appear to be molded to his athletic physique. His golden brown hair is always impeccably styled, and his presence is accompanied by an aura of quiet confidence and authority.

As the illegitimate son of a powerful mafia don, Rivaan has been groomed from a young age to take over the family business. He has proven himself to be ruthless, cunning and intelligent, earning the respect and fear of his peers..

However, Rivaan was already obsessed with *The La Regine Della*. Rivaanis obsession with *La Regina Della* has become an all-consuming force in his life. He is drawn to her power and his enigmatic nature. But he wasn't aware who she really was. He was so impressed with her work. And wondered how A single woman managed to handle a huge mafia empire. His gaze softened, when he saw bliss for the first time at the party, it gave him an idea that *The La Regina Dell* might look like her. But when he got to know that Adira is the La Regina Della, he made her the aim of his life.

# CHAPTER 3

## The La Regina Della

After half an hour, I left the party. I was in my car while my driver was going back home. I was so tense, suddenly I got a call from Zara. I hurriedly picked it up and asked *"Everything alright?"*

*"Mmm...actually that doesn't seem so. Please come fast."*

And the call dropped. Now, I had asked my driver to drive fast, he was now driving insanely fast. Within fifteen minutes, I reached my home. I got out of the car hurriedly and rushed inside. I stopped in the living room, where Zara and other Eves were present. Everyone in the living room was quiet and tense.

*"What happened ?"* I asked, but nobody replied. Then I asked, *"Where is my brother ? Where's Krish ?"* still I got no reply. I then rushed to Krish's room without waiting for a reply and, when I opened up the door of his room, and, I no longer felt the floor under my feets. There was blood all over the floor of his room. I just wasn't able to believe my eyes. I took my heels out and went inside his room. And checked his bathroom with the hope that I might find him there. But there was just no sign of him, except the window of his room was broken. My eyes filled with tears, I was trying hard

to control my emotions. Then I came back to the living room.,

*"Please just tell me Zara, where's my brother."*

She looked at me with a guilt in her eyes. And no longer was able to control my anger and my crying, and I burst out screaming. *"Where is my fucking brother ? You were here, all the time with him. Where the fuck is he ?"* I cried.

*"Adira, I'm so so sorry. You left him sleeping, but when I went to check on him, he wasn't there. He was nowhere to be found. It's my fault. It's all my fault."* Zara started crying.

*"But you might have heard some noises ? Any kind of noise ? Scattering of the window ? No?"*

*"No."*

Now, I started having a headache. I grabbed my head. While Zara cried and repeated, *"It's all my fault. It's all my fault..."*

*"No."* I shouted. *"It is your fault but don't repeat it."*

I leaned against the wall and sat down. I started taking deep breaths to control my emotions. Just then my phone rang. It was Lennox. Suddenly his words popped up in my mind. But, I picked up the call. I didn't bother myself to say anything, I was ready to listen.

*"How's the surprise ? Good enough ?"* My eyes widened. How can I miss this ?

*"Adira, I never try to acquire anything without knowing 'bout it. I was always aware of your Nova Spire. Now, let's play rough. Adira."*

*""You want to play rough? I'll redefine brutality.""*

*"Ah-ha ? That's the real Adira. The La Regina Della."*

And I hung up the call.

It was quite easy for me to find my brother and kill Lennox. But only if Lennox was the one to control the Raos. There was someone behind the veil. He was controlling Raos indirectly. He just needed a puppet, so that he can always be someone unrevealed. He was so intelligent, smart and so clever. He was only known by his alias, *'The mastermind'* Nobody can meet him unless he wants to meet that person. I knew that I would never be able to find my brother alone. I needed the support of someone as powerful as Mastermind. But I wondered why someone would take enmity with Mastermind.

So, Zara advised me to first check the areas of all the mafias.

*"I think you should go to the mafias, by yourself and ask their permission to check."*

*"Yeah. you're right. So, to whom are we going ?"*

*"So...we'll start with...Rivaan."*

*"Who's him?"*

*"A mafia. He's the young, with as much power as the mastermind."*

*"It's amazing how powerful he is at such a young age. His parents must be really powerful."*

*"Yeah."*

Then we got into the car to meet Rivaan. We left for his hub, *The Raven Hurst*. When I was in the car, I was so nervous, am I really going to ask for permission from a teenager. Though that would be so embarrassing, I would still have to do it, for the sake of my brother. I never talked to any teenager, except my brother.

*"What would I say to that kid ? What if he asks for something. What if he doesn't know anything about, about what decision he should make."*

*"Wait. What did you say ? asks for something ?"*

*"Yeah. I mean what should I expect from a teenager."*

*"Oh, my bad...I let my erotica thoughts win."*

*"Gosh, you're so double minded."*

*"He's a Nice guy, I guess."*

*"Uh-ha ? nice guys don't go be mafia."*

Soon, the imposing gates of The Raven Hurst loomed into view, a stark contrast to the urban grit we'd just left behind. A sense of unease, a familiar prickling of my senses, began to surface as the car crunched to a halt on the gravel driveway. It was a feeling I associated with places of power, places where secrets festered beneath a veneer of civility.

We got out of the car, the silence of the estate pressing in on us. I took a look around, my gaze sweeping over the scene, cataloging details, assessing the atmosphere. The Raven Hurst was a sprawling mansion, its dark stone walls exuding an air of ancient wealth and brooding isolation. It was nestled amidst a vast expanse of manicured lawns and towering trees, a secluded fortress hidden from the outside world.

The architecture was Gothic, with sharp angles, pointed arches, and an abundance of gargoyles that seemed to leer down from the rooftops. It was beautiful, in a forbidding, almost menacing way. There was a stillness to the air, an absence of the usual sounds of life, that felt unnatural. Even the wind seemed to hold its breath as it whispered through the trees.

I couldn't shake the feeling that I was being watched, that unseen eyes were observing our arrival. The Raven Hurst felt like a place where shadows held secrets, and the very stones held the weight of untold stories. It was a place that both intrigued and unsettled me, a place where I knew, instinctively, that nothing was quite as it seemed.

# CHAPTER 4
## Rauf

As I got the news, that Zara and Adira arrived. I went out to welcome them. That was the first time ever, women had arrived in the Raven Hurst. Every member of our gang was equally surprised. We all wondered what could be the reason for them to arrive. Keeping these thoughts aside, I welcomed them warm heartedly and invited them inside. And gave them a good hospitality.

*"Thank you so much for your hospitality...Mr..."* Adira said.

*"Rauf Miroslava."* I replied.

*"Yeah. Mr. Rauf. Thank you. But we came here for some extremely important work. So, will you please call Rivaan, If he's not busy. So that I can have a few words with him."*

I was stunned. I should've expected this. I paused, then I said. *"Yes, why not ."*

Then I left Adira and Zara in the living room, and rushed to Rivaan. I was so happy and excited. *"Rivaan. Rivaan."* I shouted.

He was in his control room, attending a meeting. When he heard me calling out his name, he muted his mike. I reached the control room, I was panting and smiling at the same time. He was looking at me, with no expression on his face.

*"I told you not to disturb me. It was an important meeting."*

*"Rivaan, it's not the time for a meeting. She's here."*

*"What ? what a 'she' must be doing here ?"*

*"Just come with me."*

*"What happened ?"*

*"As soon as possible."*

I grabbed his hand and pulled him with me. And I left his hand near the living room. He then started fixing his wrist watch and he was coming towards the living room. Adira was already standing, scanning the room. And Rivaan entered, he was still fixing his wrist watch, not aware of who was standing in front of him. The moment he lifted his head up to see who was that 'she' was, his jaw dropped to find Adira waiting for him. He stopped breathing, he was just glaring at Adira. The clear words coming out of Adira's lips were blurring by the time they reached Rivaan's ears.

# CHAPTER 5

## The La Regina Della

I noticed. I was surprised that he wasn't a teenager, but a young, handsome man, his 6 '6 height and golden eyes forced me not to look away. But I soon felt a little irritated because he was looking at me and he wasn't saying anything, was there something on my face ? I stood quiet there now. I stood paused, my silver eyes gleaming like polished steel. The sun setting outside,. cast a warm glow, through the window, illuminating my face and sending a shaft of light directly into Rivaan's golden eyes.

I sensed his gaze. My silver eyes narrowed, I turned my expression unreadable. Rivaan might have felt a shiver run down his spine as I began to walk towards him, my heels clicking on the marble floor. The air was electric with tension as we faced each other, our eyes locked in silent challenge.

Then Rauf, hit Rivaan with his elbow, and Rivaan came back to his senses. He then vocalised his throat to speak, He inhaled and said, *"I...I apologize for my behaviour."*

*"No... problem"* I said.

After a pause, Rivaan said, *"Please sit down."*

Me, and Zara sat down and I started. *"Sorry to disturb you. But It was important.."*

*"You don't have to apologize".*

*"Okay. so the thing is, I need to check on your area"*

*"You're free to check".*

I paused, because he didn't even bother to hesitate or ask, and I thought I would have to give him a long explanation. Then I said, *"Thank you so much. "*

*"But, what is the matter?"*

I paused again to think whether to tell him or not, *"Lennox kidnapped my brother."*

*"I hope we can find at least someone related to Lennox in my area. But are you sure you can find your brother alone?"*

*"Actually no."*

Rivaan came close to me and grabbed my hands and said.

*"Let me help you."*

This unexpected offer threw me off balance. *"But why...?"* The question escaped my lips before I could stop it, laced with suspicion.

His gaze held mine, surprisingly earnest. *"Please, I'm insisting."* There was a strange intensity in his eyes, a determination that went beyond mere politeness. It was almost...compelling. But I couldn't shake the feeling that there was more beneath the surface.

*"But why you wanna make a new rival?"* The words were out before I could fully process them. It was the most logical explanation, wasn't it? Rivaan thrived on competition, on having adversaries to test his strength against. Helping me, someone clearly in a precarious position, seemed counterintuitive unless he saw some future benefit in our conflict.

A shadow flickered across his features, but it was gone as quickly as it appeared. *"That really doesn't matter."* His tone was dismissive, as if my concerns were insignificant. It only deepened my suspicion. Nothing Rivaan did was without reason.

*Despite the lingering doubts, a fragile tendril of hope unfurled within me."*

*"Oh. I'm so grateful. Thank you so much, Rivaan."*

*"You better call me, Riaan. And believe me, It's my pleasure."*

I gave him a gentle smile, and Rivaan smiled back. Rauf interrupted. "*So, let's get to work. Nova 11, it's a building in our area. We suspect that people who know Lennex work there.*"

"*Rauf will take you guys there.*" Rivaan said.

The journey to Nova 11 was a blur of tense silence and the low hum of the vehicles. Zara sat beside me, her gaze fixed out the window, while Rauf, flanked by several of Rivaan's men, exuded an air of quiet authority. Leaving Raven Hurst felt like stepping into a different kind of danger, a more corporate, less overtly brutal landscape.

Soon, the imposing, sleek structure of Nova 11 pierced the skyline. As we arrived, a palpable shift occurred. The moment we stepped out of the vehicles, the people milling about – employees, security – seemed to freeze. Every head turned, and a wave of something that felt like a mixture of respect and stark fear rippled through the crowd. Their eyes darted between Rauf and the armed men accompanying us, and a hushed stillness fell over the usually bustling entrance. It was a stark display of Rivaan's reach, even into this seemingly legitimate corporation.

We moved with purpose, Rauf leading the way, directly towards what I assumed was the director's office. There was no challenge, no hesitation from anyone we encountered. Doors seemed to open before us, and whispers followed in our wake. The power Rivaan wielded was suffocating, extending its tendrils into every corner of this city.

The director's office was sterile and modern, a stark contrast to the dark opulence of Raven Hurst. The man behind the large glass desk looked pale and visibly nervous as Rauf addressed him, his voice carrying an unmistakable weight of command. "*I want your 7 best employees.*"

The director didn't even attempt to argue, his eyes flickering nervously between Rauf and the silent, imposing figures surrounding him. He clearly understood the unspoken threat. A simple denial wasn't an option. With a trembling hand, he reached for an intercom, issuing swift, clipped instructions. Within minutes, seven individuals, looking equally apprehensive and confused, were ushered into the office. Rauf gave them a cursory glance, a silent assessment, before nodding curtly. The director, visibly relieved, simply handed them over, his eyes pleading with them to comply.

The return journey to Raven Hurst was equally swift and silent, the seven new additions riding with a palpable tension. Now, they were meant to go with

Zara and me. Before we parted ways to head towards Nova Spire, a question gnawed at me. I turned to Rauf, his expression unreadable. *"Why did you ask about the 7 best employees?"*

He gave a small, knowing smile, a hint of something shrewd in his eyes. *"Well, Adira, Lennox have really good connections with the CEO, founder, and director of company Nova 11. Everyone who wants to be at the best position in that company, first has to go to Lennox and work for him, impress him. The best employee here is the best man from Lennox."* His words painted a clear picture. Lennox wasn't just a name; he was a kingmaker within Nova 11. These seven individuals weren't just skilled workers; they were Lennox's chosen, his most trusted. This added a whole new layer of complexity to our mission. It wasn't just about accessing Nova Spire; it was about navigating the intricate web of Lennox's influence.

*"Thank you so much, Rauf."*

*"I'd like to work with you. See you soon."*

*"Sure."*

The decision was made swiftly. There was no time for sentimentality. Lennox's connections within Nova 11 were the key, and these seven individuals were the fastest route to unlocking that information. Zara and I made our preparations quickly, a silent understanding passing between us.

Then I left for Nova Spire, with Zara. The seven employees, their initial confusion likely escalating into fear, were efficiently secured. There was no need for unnecessary brutality, but there was also no room for hesitation. Their hands were bound behind their backs with tight restraints, and black cloths were firmly tied around their heads, plunging them into disorienting darkness. Their muffled protests were ignored; our purpose was singular and unwavering.

Leading them out to the waiting vehicles felt clinical, almost detached. They were simply assets, tools to be used to achieve our goal. There was no personal animosity, no pleasure taken in their predicament. It was a necessary step, a calculated move in a game where information was the most valuable currency.

As we drove towards Nova Spire, I glanced at the silent, bound figures in the back. Their fear was palpable, a thick tension that filled the confined space. Did I feel remorse? Not in the slightest. They were obstacles, albeit human ones, standing between me and what I needed to know. Their comfort was irrelevant. Their lives, if they proved uncooperative, were equally so.

The thought of extracting the information, by whatever means necessary, was a cold, pragmatic calculation in my mind. If they willingly provided what we sought, their ordeal would end. If not... well, I had dealt with far more resistant individuals in the past. The ease with which their lives could be extinguished was a simple truth, a reality I had long accepted. They were employees, not hardened criminals, but in this world, survival depended on ruthlessness, and I had long since mastered that particular skill. Nova Spire awaited, and these seven would either be the key to unlocking its secrets or simply another footnote in the brutal tapestry of my life.

**Nova Spire,** A huge labyrinth. It was a massive, outdoor labyrinth with towering walls made of cold, gray stone. The walls were approximately 80 feet high. At the centre of the Nova Spire to was a huge mansion known as hub, with multiple paths converging toward it.

When we reached, we made all the seven employees stand in a corner of the lobby. Of Nova Spire. The night passed. Next day we removed the cloth from the head of the employees. After that we left them in a completely empty corner. Then me and Zara went to the hub.

*"What are you gonna do with 'em ?"*

*"Eventually they all have to die."*

*"I mean what are you gonna ask them ? Where is Krish or Lennox ?"*

*"No. Not Krish. They might not be aware of Krish but Lennox."*

*"But what if they are not even aware of Lennox.*

*"To lick his ass, they have to meet him in person, I just need to know the spot."*

*"Can we do the interrogation later and just eat something ? I'm starving right now."*

*"Why not."*

Then while we were going in the kitchen, I got a call from an unknown number. I picked it up hurriedly. Hoping for Krish, when I placed the phone on my ear, I heard Krish screaming. They were torturing him. And he was begging. And the call disconnected.. I stood there for a moment while breathing heavily in anger. my hands were shivering in frustration. I had to release my anger on someone. Then I went to the weapon room. Zara followed me. I was walking so fast.

And as I got to the room I slammed the door. The weapon room is also called The Armory.

# THE ARMORY, It was a secure facility designed for the storage and maintenance of firearms, tactical equipment, with reinforced walls, a secure door, and advanced surveillance systems to ensure the safekeeping of sensitive materials.

As I slammed the door of the Armory, I paused and looked around to find my axe hanging between the manual weapons.

## Crimson Requiem, an alias of my axe. This battle worn axe has been the trusty companion of its wielder through countless battles and gruesome murders. The axe's broad black curve blade, forged from the finest high carbon steel, has been honed to a razor's edge, Its surface detached with a lattice of fine lines, a testament to the countless lives it has claimed

I picked the Crimson Requiem, and started walking out of the hub. Zara followed me till she guessed the purpose of me going towards the employee. I stopped at a distance, when I saw those 7 employees talking to each other. Then I ran towards them. And in the blink of an eye, I dissected the neck of one of the employees. The head was continuously rolling until I stopped it with my leg and placed my foot on that head. The rest of the employees went silent. I was breathing heavily and turned towards Zara and smiled. I was satisfied. Soon my smile turned into a laugh. And again I turned to the employees and stopped laughing.

Then I made all of the 6 employees sit down on their knees. And placed my axe on the trapezius (a body part between the shoulder and the neck) of one of the employees. And asked him about Lennox. He said he didn't know, so I didn't bother to ask again, and I just dissected his head. I did the same for the rest of the 5 employees. I would simply ask one time and dissect the heads.

I killed 3 more employees. They were really not aware about Lennox at that time. Now two employees were left. They told me that they can tell me something else, useful to me. He said, "*Finnick, Lennox's dealer. He supplies energy drugs and power medicines to all the Raos. Especially* **Therons**. *You should go to Moscow. Then go to the main Brothel area. Then ask the head Brothel, say to her, that, 3rd door 1976. She'll take you to Finnick. And if you want to take him with you, say 'LA9'.*"

Raos, They were divided into three parts. The mafia gangs are divided into two parts, to kill and to be killed. But Raos was divided into three parts, **THE KAMIKAZE**, this name tells its own meaning. This part exists to be killed, no families to take care of. not to kill, Lennox and the Mastermind, was their lord. Lennox uses them to provoke the opponent to attack, whenever they want a long enmity. But still the Kamikazes used to have weapons like knives as swords, but never a gun. **THE ONA VIIRS**, their work was to kill and to be killed. They were provided with guns and knives but never with helmets or bullet proof jackets. They were not even specially trained to protect themselves and to kill. They were just simple killers And here it comes, **The THERONS**, They were just to kill, not to be killed. They were highly trained. And were provided with hightech machines and guns, they had the ability to bear the electric shocks, and could hold their breath up to 25 minutes straight.

Then I gave my axe to Zara, and asked her to give 1 million dollars to both the employees.

On that same day, I orchestrated another move. I sent some of my most trusted operatives – the "eves," as I called them – with Zara to Moscow. There was another piece to this puzzle, a vital one named Finnick, and Moscow was where he resided. While I waited at Nova Spire for Zara's return with him, a sense of obligation, however twisted, compelled me to make a call.

I dialed Rivaan's number. It was, in a way, my duty to inform him. After all, it was his initial leverage, his information, that had led me to Finnick in the first place. When he answered, his voice a low rumble, I laid it out plainly. I told him about Finnick, about my plans to bring him to Nova Spire. Then, almost as an afterthought, I asked if he wanted to join me. A strange impulse, perhaps a desire to see his reaction, or maybe a subconscious acknowledgment of his unexpected assistance. He agreed without hesitation, a flicker of something akin to anticipation in his tone.

It wasn't long before Zara's vehicle pulled up to Nova Spire. A wave of relief washed over me – another piece was falling into place. She brought Finnick out of the car with a surprising degree of gentleness. There were no restraints visible, no signs of struggle. Zara, ever the pragmatist, likely opted for a more diplomatic approach.

Her surprise was evident when she saw Rivaan standing beside me, a silent, imposing presence. Her eyes flickered between us, a question forming on her lips that she wisely chose not to voice.

Before fully extracting Finnick from the vehicle, Zara leaned in, her voice low and persuasive. I saw her offer him a black cloth strip. She was requesting his cooperation, a move that spoke of her efficiency. Why resort to force if compliance could be achieved with a simple request?

However, Finnick's reaction was far from cooperative.

*"Who the fuck do you think you are? Let me talk to Lennox."*

*"Sir. It's crucial."*

*"You better not tell me what is crucial and what is not."*

*"Sir, listen to me Lennox had been stuck in some enmity, that's why, you're not supposed to see his exact location...For your safety measures."*

*"Oh ...You should have told me before."*

Then Zara tied that black cloth on his eyes and took him in a special room, It was a dimly lit torture room. Stark, soulless space that reeked of desperation and fear. But there was a window through which some sunlight could be seen. A single flickering overhead bulb costeerie shadows on the floor. Rusty metal pipes hung menacingly from the ceiling and a stained wooden chair stood ominously in the centre of the room. There were some other comfortable chair in that room for the one who will torture the other person .

As Zara made him sit there, she took off the cloth from Finnick's eyes and then Finnick opened up his eyes and saw me and Rivaan sitting there in front of him. And there were eves around the room. I had asked Rivaan to talk to Finnick.

"*Where's Lennox and who are you ?*" Finick asked with confusion.

"*I'm Rivaan and she's Adira.*" Rivaan replied.

Finnick's aggressive reply hung in the air, a sudden shift in the dynamic. He leaned back against the car seat, his voice laced with suspicion and a newfound defiance. *"Wait. I think I've heard 'bout you guys..."* His eyes, though I couldn't see them clearly beneath the offered blindfold, seemed to be assessing us, piecing together fragments of information he'd likely overheard in the underworld.

Rivaan, ever the opportunist, stepped forward, a predatory gleam in his golden eyes. *"Good, We are Lennox's rivals."* He stated it with a chilling certainty, a clear declaration of allegiance – or rather, opposition.

Finnick's head tilted slightly, a flicker of intrigue replacing his initial irritation. *"Means you're not by Lennox's side?"* The question was sharp, probing. He was trying to understand the power structure at play, to gauge where his own interests might lie.

I remained silent, letting Rivaan take the lead for now.

*"When did I say that?"* Rivaan countered smoothly, a dangerous edge to his voice. He enjoyed these verbal sparring matches, the subtle dance of intimidation and manipulation.

Finnick hesitated for a moment, then his voice hardened. *"Only he or his people knew the code to call me."* He was laying down his own terms, establishing his importance. He wasn't just some random contact; he was protected, connected.

*"Okay, so, now, we know it too."* Rivaan's reply was dismissive, brushing aside Finnick's attempt at leverage as if it were nothing. He had a way of making others feel insignificant with just a few words.

A beat of silence passed. Finnick, likely considering his options, finally spoke, his tone shifting to a more pragmatic one. *"Look, I'm a dealer, I work for money. And I have nothing to do with your and Lennox's personal matters."* He was drawing a clear line, positioning himself as a neutral party motivated solely by profit.

Rivaan's gaze sharpened, his patience wearing thin. *"so... you're saying that you want money to open your mouth."* It wasn't a question, but a statement, laced with a hint of disdain.

*"Well. Yes."* Finnick admitted readily, his earlier aggression replaced by a shrewd calculation. He knew his worth, and he wasn't afraid to name his price.

*"Okay. Then you tell me whatever you know about him."* Rivaan conceded, his tone indicating that this was a necessary, albeit distasteful, transaction.

Finnick paused again, the silence stretching, thick with anticipation. Then, he finally spoke, a new layer of complexity entering his voice. *"But I have a condition..."*

Now me and Rivaan both got irritated and I muttered, *"Fuck his conditions."* and turned my face towards the wall.

*"What is it ?"* Rivaan asked.

*"I'll tell everything to only one of you present in this room and in French."*

Rivaan looked at me for consent and I signaled him to talk to Finnick. *"I know French, You can speak."*

When he said that, I looked at Zara, and Zara looked at me. Then Zara gave me a can of cold coffee and I started drinking it. Then Finnick started talking to Rivaan in French. Then in the middle of the conversation, Rivaan looked at me and signaled me. Then I stood with coffee in my hands. And I walked till the corner of the torture room and grabbed a spear that was kept in the corner of the room. Then I came behind Finnick while he was talking to Rivaan. I suddenly tossed the spear and thrusted it into

Finnick's head, and blood flowed from his head like a waterfall. In the blink of an eye, he became lifeless and took a sip of coffee. Rivaan who was sitting in front of Finnick, his white shirt drenched in Finnick's blood, and he sighed. Everybody in that room was standing still and calm like nothing had happened.

After everyone came out of that room, Rivaan was about to sit in his car to leave, But then he stopped, and turned to me, I was standing behind Rivaan.

*"Why didn't you ask me what he said ?"*

I paused and made a confused face and replied," *Maybe... because I trust you. So if anything important he has said you would've told me."*

Then Rivaan smiled *"Finding Krish, it's on me now"*.

And then Rivaan left. I watched him leave and then I felt how lucky I was that I met a man like Rivaan.

# NEXT DAY

My phone rang, the sudden shrill tone jolting me out of my preoccupied state. I glanced at the screen. Rivaan's name flashed across the display. A wave of confusion washed over me. I picked up the phone, holding it to my ear. "*Rivaan?*" My voice held a note of cautious inquiry, mirroring the uncertainty swirling within me. What new development,

"*Will you do me a favour ?*"

"*Yeah.*"

"*Can you go to Moscow with some Eves to find a bike with the number plate I just sent you on your phone ?Don't worry. It won't waste your time. Please leave right now.*"

"*Okay.*"

Then I left for Moscow on that same day with Zare and some eves. Moscow falls under Rivaan's area. The city was busy as usual as well as the roads. All the eves were spreaded all over the city. And on a really random road. I came and stood in the middle of the road. It was a bit rainy and I was wearing a black raincoat. And my face was covered with a cap attached to the raincoat. As I went and stood in the middle of that busy road, every vehicle was ignoring me and was moving so fast. And some of them were asking me to be aside until.......I removed that attached cap...Everybody stopped and went silent, a complete silence. Then I ordered the eves that were with me to check the number plate. But then a bike rider in between the random vehicles increased the speed of the bike when he saw me. I noticed it and asked one to check the number plate of that bike. Then the biker increased the speed so much that it was impossible to stop the bike unless it gets bumped into something. As the eves went near to that biker, the biker rode the bike right away. Then I took the bike of one eve and followed the biker. As I weaved through the crowded Moscow street on my sleek black motorcycle, my eyes remained fixed on my target. I expertly navigated his bike through the chaos, my long black hair whipping behind me like a black banner. Suddenly, I spotted an opportunity to cut off the biker and took a sharp turn down a narrow street branched off to my right. It was a square shaped street. My bike's tyres screeched on the pavement, and suddenly found myself facing a second even narrower street that branched off to my left. That's when I saw a man clad in a long, black coat and hat, standing motionless in the shadows. His hand gripped a sturdy stick, which seemed innocuous enough until he clicked a hidden button, and a gleaming blade sprang out from the stick's base, transforming it into a deadly axe. My instincts screamed warning as the man began to move towards me, his eyes glinting with malice. With a swift, menacing motion, the man swung the axe at me. With lighting, quick reflexes, I bend backward, my body folding like a supple willow branch. The axe whistled past my face, cutting my hair flex, mere inches from my skin, as I expertly avoided the attack. For a fleeting moment, we both locked eyes, our gazes burning. And I increased the speed of the bike to get out of the street. I took a left last turn and now I came out of the street and back on the road. I was now closer to that biker. My motorcycle roared as I gained speed. As I closed in, I swiftly pulled out my gun and fired, but the biker's protective gear rendered hard-armar jackets and level 3rd helmet, the shot ineffective. Undeterred, I retained a small, sharp knife from my stiletto strike shoes, in which the knife was attached, and accelerated, expertly maneuvering my bike to ride alongside the biker. With a swift, precise motion, I plugged the knife into the biker's thigh, causing him to lose control .The biker's bike skidded widely, dragging him along the pavement as I sped past. Then I stopped my bike and came to the biker. Sat down next to him and I called Rivaan. Rivaan told me that the biker might be carrying a well secured black suitcase. I had to give that suitcase to Rivaan . It was a little surprising for me . But I didn't think about this that much and took that suitcase. And I left the biker alive.

# CHAPTER 6
## The La Regina Della

Next day, Rivaan was waiting for me, so that he could take that suitcase, outside my mansion. When I was going out of my mansion with the suitcase and Zara, to meet Rivaan. I asked Zara,

*"By the way, what do you think about Rivaan ?"*

*"Oh. Rivaan? Yeah, he's fine."*

*"Oh. Shut up, he's more than fine.."*

*"Oh, like that.."*

*"Huh ?"*

*"Nothing. Is it hurting ?"*

*"What ?"*

*"Falling for Rivaan."*

*"I'm not falling for him... maybe."*

*"Oh, yeah ?!"*

Just in that much we reached to Rivaan. Then I gave the suitcase to Rivaan, and then he thanked me. Rivaan said, *" Well, I got a return gift for you."*

*"Uh-ha ?"*

Then, two gang members of Rivaan, brought a skinny, bald and pale man. He was so skinny that he wasn't able to stand on his own. He was a drug addict. He had a few tattoos on his body and a black leather collar or lease in his neck. His lips were black as well as his eyelids, Rivaan told me that this person's name was Alexis. And he will tell me whatever I want to know. Zara took Alexis inside the mansion. Now Rivaan and I were standing, alone. I asked him with a gesture of gratitude.

*"Is there any way I can thank you ?"*

*"Yes, just a question. "*

*"Go ahead."*

*"Okay, So, on a scale from one to ten, how bad of an idea do you think it would be if we get married ?"*

I smirked and asked, *"Are you proposing to me ?"*

*"Nah, it was just a simple question."*

*"Off the chart."*

Then Rivaan smirked.

Then after some conversation Rivaan left. And Alexis was shifted to Nova Spire. And he was locked up in a lock up. After some time, I came to talk to Alexis in the lock up. Alexis was cowered into the corner, his sunken eyes darting widely as I entered the room. My presence was imposing.

Alexis was sitting half naked on the ground with his legs crossed. I took a wooden chair, which was kept inside that lock up And kept it before Alexis and sat before him. My voice was low and even, but it carried an undercurrent of menace as she began to question Alexis.

*"So, Alexis, I hear you've been associating with some...unsavory characters. Specifically, I'm interested in anything you might know about Lennox."*

Alexis's eye flickered and he licked his dry cracked lips

*"I, I don't know what you're talking about,"* he stammered, his voice barely above a whisper. My expression remained impassive, but my eyes narrowed slightly.

*"Don't play dumb, Alexis. What could I expect from a ruined ex-Rao?"*

Here, I was expecting an answer and I waited for it.

*"the codes, safe places and internal, external affairs with few secrets"*

"Exactly."

*"How about I tell you something more valuable? What do you think, why Lennox attacked your Nova Spire ? Think about it, Adira. Your well-wishers aren't your well wishers"*

Then Alexis gave me some names. At that time I felt betrayed, when I got to know that my well-wishers were actually working for Lennox's. Those people were the business people personally knowing me.

Then I stood up silently and came out of the locker without saying even a word. I then sighed and called one eve standing there. "Come here" and as the eve came close to me, I placed my one hand on his shoulder.

*"I want all of them...on the terrace...of OKO Tower. Am I clear?"*

"Yes mam."

Then the next day, All the well-wishers were brought on the terrace of the OKO tower. The OKO tower's rooftop terrace offered a breathtaking panorama of

Moscow's cityscape, but the atmosphere tense with anticipation.

The well-wishers (betrayers) stood tensely on the rooftop, their minds racing with anxiety. They exchanged nervous glances, wondering why they had been brought to thin Secluded location and what fat had in share for here At they heard the distant when of helicopter blades, this apprehension turned to fears the sound grow louder and louder, and soon my sleek, black helicopter descended onto the rooftop, casting a menacing shadow over the scene. The well-wishers' eyes widened as I stepped out of the helicopter, my imposing figure amplified by the big, boom furry coat that enveloped here the caches thick, plush for ripped in the wind giving me an aura of untamed power. My legs were chad in sleek, black boots that added several inches to my height, making me tower over the bounded figures before me.

The boots' high heels clicked sharply on the rooftop's surface, echoing through the nightair (cold winds). My dark hair was pulled back, revealing my sharp, angular features, which were set in a determined expression. My eyes gleamed with a fierce intensity, my gaze piercing as I surveyed the rooftop scene before me. My gaze then swept over the well-wishers, my expression unreadable, as I began to stride towards them with deliberate, measured steps. With every step I took, the beat of the well-wishers' heart was also increasing.

As I stepped close to the bound figures, my eyes scanned the group with a mixture of disdain and curiosity. I stopped in front of one of the well-wishers, a scrawny man with trembling lips. My gaze bore into his.

With a deliberate slowness, I bent towards the man, my face inches from his. My voice was bow and menacing, sending shivers down the spines of the other well-wishers.

"*Why ?*" I whispered, my breath caressing the man's ear. "*Why did you choose to pledge your loyalty to Lennox?*" The well-wisher's eyes darted widely, searching for an escape or a reprieve . He swallowed hard, his Adam's apple bobbing up and down. '*H-He is terrifying.*"

My expression didn't change but my eyes seemed to bore deeper into his soul. *"Terrifying ?...Than me ?"* I asked.

*"No, w-we were promised protection"* he stammered. *"Lennox, promised power and safety."* My expression remained the same. *"Protection?"* I repeated, my voice dripping with skepticism. *"Power? You think Lennox can offer you anything that I couldn't?"*

Then man's eyes dropped, and he mumbled Something incoherent. My gaze lingered on a moment before I straightened up, my eyes scanning the group.

*'I see."* I said, my voice dripping with disappointment. *"You all thought you could betray me and get away with it. But you forgot one thing: I am Adira. The La Regina Della. And I always collect my debts."*

I paused, letting the weight of my words sink in. *"Now you will have to burn...in the fire of my vengeance."* As I ordered, I widened my eyes, my eyelids rising in a dramatic, exaggerated motion. My eyebrows arched giving me an air of mocking surprise. A sly mischievous glint danced in my eyes, sparkling with amusement.

I gave a sarcastic smile, the corners of my mouth twitching upward. The smile was a thin, mirthless life, devoid of genuine warmth or humor. Instead, it conveyed a sense of mocking regret.

The bound figures exchanged terrified glancer, their minds racing with the implication of my words, they knew they had crossed a line, and now they would have to pay the price.

Then I gave a clever, teasing smile to the group but instantly turned cold and unforgiving. I turned towards one Eve, my voice devoid of emotion. *"Burn them alive."* my eyes glinting with a fierce intensity.

The well-wishers' eyes widened in horror as my words hung in the air like a death sentence. Their faces turned ashen, drained of all color, as they struggled to comprehend the magnitude of their fate.

Some of them screamed, their voices piercing nightair (nightair- cold winds) like shattered glass. Others begged, their pleas falling from trembling lips like desperate prayers.

One of them, a burly man with a thick beard stumbled forward, his eyes wild with terror, *"No, Adira, please!"*

he begged his voice cracking with desperation. *"We'll do anything! Just spare our lives."*

After hearing this line, I came closer to that man, bent toward him. And narrowed my eyes and said, *"oh, really? Then I want you to die."* Then I got up, turned and walked away. I climbed into my helicopter and sat in that, watching the group begging.

Their cries and pleas forming a chaotic cacophony that echoed off the rooftop. But my expressions remained unmoved, my eyes glinting with a cold, unforgiving light.

The Eves, however, moved with a swift efficiency, their faces impassive as they doused the betrayers with flammable liquid. The air was heavy with the stench of gasoline, and the betrayers' screams grew more frantic as they realized their fate was sealed.

As I watched, my expression remained impassive. I reached into my matte black handbag and pulled out a pair of sleek, black Valentino glasses.

With a deliberate slowness, I placed the glasses on my face, my eyes now hidden behind the black shades seemed to gleam with an added a layer of sophistication and ruthlessness.

As the flammable liquid's glow illuminated the rooftop, my voice calmed and detached, *"Let's go."* I said, my words directed at the pilot.

The helicopter's rotors whirred to life, and the aircraft lifted off into the sky. My gaze lingered on the rooftop for a moment, my eyes hidden in my glasses. Then, I turned away, my attention focused on the city.

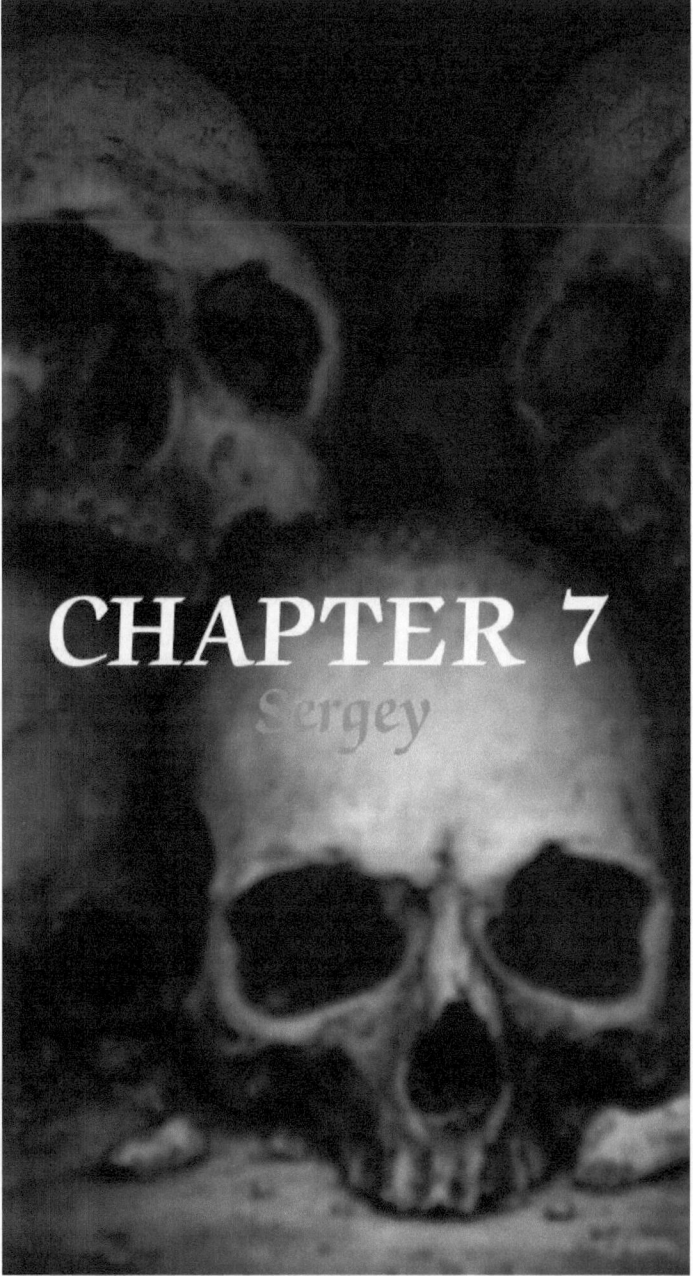

# CHAPTER 7
## Sergey

**(I'm Sergey. One of the eve. I was present at the roof of the OKO tower, when Mam Adira ordered to burn the well wishers.)**

As the helicopter begins to disappear into the distance. The eves, including me, ensured the betrayers were fully engulfed in the flames. We watched for a movement, making sure the job was done before turning to leave.

As we descended the staircase, the sound of screams and wailing blue louder. The well wishers now engulfed in flames, stumbled and fell, their bodies crashing to the rooftop.

Some of them, ablaze and frantic, stumble toward the edge of the rooftop, their schemes a queen through the night air. They toppled over the edge, falling through the brightness, their bodies silhouetted against the daylight.

The sound of crunching metal and shattered glass filled the air as some of the following bodies landed on the hoods or loops of huge vehicles and trucks, parked below. The impact was sickening, the vehicles alarms blaring in discordant harmony with the screams of burning betrayers.

Others, still ablaze, rolled and tumbled across the rooftop, their flames flickering widely as they desperately tried to extinguish the inferno consuming their bodies. The air was heavy with the acrid smell of burning flash and the sound of anguished screams.

The Eves, including me, meanwhile, disappeared, leaving behind a scene of utter Carnage and devastation. The rooftop, once a symbol of power and luxury, was now a charnel house, gruesome testament to my ruthless vengeance.

The people in the surrounding buildings and on the streets below were shocked and horrified by the scene unfolding before their eyes. Some screamed and covered their mouths, while others should frozen in terror, unable to look away.

Cars screeched to a halt on the streets below, their drivers and passengers staring up at the rooftop in disbelief. Siren began to wail in the distance, growing louder as emergency services rushed to the scene.

Panic set in as people scrambled to get away from the scene. Some ran wildly, desperate to escape the carnage, while others stood frozen unsure of what to do.

The city's day life came to an abrupt halt, the music and laughter replaced by screams and sirens. The once-vibrant streets were now a scene of chaos and terror, as people struggled to comprehend the sheer brutality of what they had just witnessed.

# CHAPTER 8
## The La Regina Della

As I descended on the rooftop of Nova Spire, the cold night air enveloped me, a stark contrast to the fiery passion that still lingered within me from the Rooftop encounters. An Eve, clad in tactical gear, emerged from the shadows, awaiting my attention.

*"Ma'am, we've cleared the old wooden furniture from the lower levels, so, shall we incinerate the remains ?"* The Eve stated, his voice low and efficient. My gaze narrowed, my mind already shifting gears.

*"Do it on the ground, away from the structure. I don't want any unwanted attention."* With a curt nod, Eve vanished, leaving me to my true objective. I strode purposely toward the detention area, my footsteps echoing through the corridors. The air was thick with the scent of disinfectant and the distant hum machinery. My heels clicking against the polished concrete floor. Finally, I arrived at Alexis' holding cell. Door sliding open with a metallic hiss. My eyes adjusted to the dim light overhead cast on an eerie glow on the sterile environment. and I beheld Alexis slumped on the floor, a cigarette dangling from his lips, the sweet, acrid scent of drugs wafting through the air.

My gaze swept the room, settling on a lone chair tucked away in a corner. With silent deliberation, I retrieved the chair and positioned it in front of Alexis, my eyes locking onto his with an unnerving intensity. *"Now what you want, Adira?"* Alexis asked , *" You know why you are here, Alexis ?"*

"*Yeah, for the information.*"

"*Then give me the fucking information. Alexis.*"

"*Oh, Yes, I know about your brother. You're smart, you're after Lennox, not your brother. Because only Lennox knows the location of your brother. But tell me, if you get the exact information about where your brother is, what would you do ?*"

"*ofcourse, I would go there.*" I answered. After hearing my reply, Alexis pause and said. *"Johny."*

"*Sins?*" Zara interrupted

"*Shut up.*" I replied angrily. ,

"*He is a smuggler.*" Alexis continued. "*Addicted to young girls.*"

"*Something kinda Sugar daddy ?*" Zara said.

"*Absolutely.*" Alexis replied. Then he continued.

*"Jony already has a ton of enemies. He is really close to Lennox and Mastermind. So the only way to reach Lennox or the Mastermind is, when they want you, to reach them. kill Johny, and they shall find you. But the Mastermind should come to know that Johnny is killed by the mastermind's rival, not by Johny's. That is all. Now this is where our journey ends, Adira. Kill him with a knife, not a gun. Today he'll be in the Krasnaya Zvezda casino."*

My eyes narrowed slightly as I thanked Alexis for the information. But before I could say something else, Alexis spoke up, a sly grin spreading across his face. *"I can make it easier for you,"* he said, in his voice dripping with malice. *"I can tell you exactly where your brother, Krish, is. But I won't."*

My expression turned cold, my voice dropping to a menacing tone *"Why not ?"*

Alexis's refusal to divulge Krish's location wasn't driven by malice, but rather by a calculated attempt to negotiate with me. He had a list of demands, and he was willing to play hardball to get what he wanted.

*"Actually, I'll tell you where Krish is,"* Alexis said, *"But first, you need to meet my terms."* I raised my eyebrows, my interest piqued, *"Oh. Terms ?"*

*"I want a 50/50 partnership with you"*, Alexis replied, his voice firm. Zara's eyes widened as she heard this. Everyone there was shocked except me. I smiled but my smile was full of frustration. Then Alexis continued. *"And I want a few tons of the most expensive drug, Hemegenix, as a token of our new partnership."*

I gave a forceful stretch on my face, *"Not even a piece of shit will be given to you."* I spat. *"Not even a penny will be given to you. And as for the partnership, you are not even worthy to breathe in the same air as in which I breathe."* I brusted.

*"Oh, be polite,"* Alexis said. Then I inhaled and exhaled in order to calm down. Then I bent towards him and said, *"Okay. So,I have a better deal. How about you tell me about my brother's location, you know it can save my time and all."*

*"And it's less risky for you too."* Zara added.

*"Yeah, that can be a point too. And in return I shall let you live you, your this little useless life."*

Alexis' smile faltered and for a moment, he looked uncertain. But then, his expression hardened, and he sneered at me. "*You'll never get what you want from me.*" hai voice dripped with defiance.

My eyes narrowed, my hand instinctively reaching for the nice at my waist. "*We'll see about that. You'll tell me what I want to know, ot you will beg for mercy. And even then, I might not spare your life.*"

"*I don't care if I live or die but I won't tell you anything.*"

My face twisted in anger. "*Then what is the use of your living ? Let's just kill you.*"

Without hesitation, I grabbed Alexis by his leash tied around his neck and dragged him across the ground. He stumbled and struggled to keep up, but my grip was unyielding.

As we approached the burning pile of old furniture. Alexis' eyes widened in terror. He realised too late what I had planned for him.

With a vicious heave, I hurdled Alexis into the heart of the fire. He screamed as the flames engulfed him, his body trashing wildly as he tried to escape The inferno.

I watched, my expression unyielding, as Alexis burned. The sounds of his screams and the crackling of the flames filled the air, a haunting melody that seemed to echo through the evening.

As I walked back to the Nova Spire, the smell of smoke and sweat clung to me. I couldn't shake off the feeling of unease, despite having dealt with Alexis.

---

Upon entering the Nova Spire, I was greeted by the familiar site of maps and strategical plans covering the walls. My team, a mic of seasons operates and young recruits, looks up at me with a mix of curiosity and concern.

*"Adira did you..."* Zara nodding towards the smell of smoke and sweat. My expression turned grim. *"Alexis won't be a problem anymore. We need to focus on Johny."*

*"Johny ?"*

*"Yeah. Johny."*

"You're believing him...Are you serious ? He's a drug addict, no way he was telling the truth."

"You know, Zara, why I never let him have the urge to sniff drugs or marijuana ?"

"Why ?"

"Because an intoxicating person, can never lie."

"So, are you leaving today ?"

"Yeah. In 20 minutes."

As I prepared to leave, Zara approached me a look of concern etched on her face. *"Adira will you ever come back ?"* she asked me her voice laced with worry.

My expression turned sombre, my eyes clouding over with a mixture of determination and uncertainty. *"I don't know."* My voice barely above a whisper. Zara's eyes widened, her grip on my arm tightened. *"What do you mean ? You cannot just leave without even knowing if you will ever return."*

I gently extricated myself from Zara's grasp, her movements economical and precise. *"It's the only way to flash out Lennox"*

Zara's face paled, her eyes darting nervously around. *"But what if they killed you at the moment ? What if we lose both you and Krish?"*

My smile was fleeting, my eyes glinting with a hint of steel. *"I'll be fine."* I said, my voice filled with confidence *"I have to do this, Zara."*

With that I turned to leave but Zara's voice stopped me in my tracks. *"Should I tell Rivaan ?"* she asked, her eyes locked on mine. My eyes flash with a warning, with a serious expression. *"Not now. When I'll be away, he'll be the one bringing Krish back home. But Zara, until I come you're in charge."* My voice was firm but gentle. Zara's eyes welled up with tears, her voice trembling. *"I don't wanna be in charge. All I want is, for you to come back safe. Nothing else matters. Promise me that you'll come...alive."*

My expression softened, my eyes filled with warmth. I placed out my warm hand on Zara's cheek, my touch gentle and reassuring. *"I promise."*

Without saying further, I held Zara's gaze for a moment, my eyes conveying a deep affection and trust. Then I turned to my sleek black Bugatti. I slid into the driver's seat of my sleek black Bugatti, the lead leather crackling to life, its headlights casting an intense glow on the surrounding darkness.

With a Swift motion, I put the car in gear and floored it. The Bugatti surged forward, its tires screeching as it devoured the distance. The speedometer needle climbed higher and higher, the wind whipping my hair into a frenzy. I quickly raised my hand, with a soft click, the Bugatti retractable roof slid smoothly into place, encasing me in a cocoon of luxury and silence.

The sudden stainless was a stark contrast to the tumultuous wind and noise of the outside world. My gaze remained fixed on the road ahead, my eyes nerode slightly as I pushed the Bugatti to its limit. As I vanished into the night, the only sound left behind was the feeding rumble of the Bugatti's engine, echoing through the darkness like a distant growl.

Soon I reached the casino. I brought the Bugatti to a smooth stop in front of the Krasnaya Zvezda casino. The tires kissing the pavement with a soft squeak. I shifted into park and killed the engine, the sudden silence a stark contrast to the roar of the engine.

The neon lights of the Russian casino Krasnaya Zvezda (means red start), glowed like a beacon in the darkness as my bugatti screeched to a halt outside the entrance, where a liveried doorman rushed to open the door of my car, I signaled him to stop. "*Я лучше сделаю это сам (I'd better do this myself)*" I said.

The casino's entrance, a grandiose affair with gleaming gold accents and crimson carpets, beckoned to me. My gaze swept the area, my eyes lingering on the burly security guards stationed at the entrance.

With a deliberate movement, I opened the door and stepped out of the car, my stiletto black book clicking on the pavement.

As I stepped into the casino, I was immediately struck by the eerie silence. The only sound was the soft hum of the chandeliers above and the muted laughter of the girls.

My eyes scanned the empty casino, my gaze lingering on the lavish decor. The big sofa, upholstered in rich velvet seemed to dominate the space, positioned as it was directly in front of the entrance door.

Johny, a fat, blad smuggler, sat on the sofa, Johny himself was a disgusting sight, surrounded by a bevy of beautiful women resplendent in their revealing outfits giggled and cooed as they fed Johny grapes and poured him champagne.

In front of the sofa, a large glass table reflected the light of the chandeliers above, casting a subtle glow over the area. The table was bare, except for a few scattered glasses and a champagne bottle chilling in a silver ice bucket.

My eyes locked onto Johny, a calculating glint sparkling within them. With a deliberate movement, I reached into my pockets and extracted a slender knife, its blade etched with the symbol of my gang.

The knife seemed to gleam in the light of the chandeliers, it's presence exuding an aura of menace. My grip on the knife, was firm. My fingers wrapping around its hilt with a practiced ease.

With the knife at my side, I began to walk towards Johny, my boots clicking on the marble floor. The sound seemed to echo through the empty casino, a steady beat that heralded my approach.

I stood tall, my feet shoulder width apart, as I positioned myself between the glass table and the sofa where Johny lounged. The knife was still clutched in my hand, its blade glinting in the light.

The air was heavy with tension as I and Johnny locked eyes. The only sound was the sofa hum of the chandeliers above as the girls also became quiet.

My movements were Swift and deadly, my knife slicing through the year with precision. In one fluid motion, I cut johny's throat. The Blade biting deep into his flash.

The girls screamed, their voices piercing the air as they scrambled to get away from the gruesome scene. Johnny's eyes widened in shock, his face contorting in agony. But I wasn't finished yet. With a Swift thrust, I plunged the knife into Johnny's left eye. The Blade sinking deep into his skull. Johnny's body jerked violently, his limbs twitching in a macabre dance before slumping lifeless against the sofa.

A girl, fueled by panic and desperation, lunged at me with the fork. But I was too quick, my reflexes honed from years of living on the edge. With a Swift motion, I grabbed the girl's wrist, my grip like a vice. "*Ah-ha, nice try.*" My voice dripping with sarcasm. The fork clattered to the floor as I pulled out my gun and pressed it against the girl's hand.

The girl's eye widened in terror as I pulled the trigger. The sound of the gunshot echoed through the casino, and the girl screamed in agony as she clutched her wounded hand.

The remaining girls cowered in fear, their eyes fixed on me with a mixture of terror and awe. My reputation as a ruthless and cunning operator was well deserved, and they knew they were no match for me.

I strode out of the casino, my heels clicking on the pavement. I slipped back into my Bugatti, the soft leather enveloping me like a glove. With a Swift motion, I started the engine, the car purring to life beneath me. My eyes scanned the rearview mirror, my gaze lingering on the casino entrance. For a moment I sat there, my fingers drumming a staccato beta on the steering wheel. Then with a sudden burst of speed, I accelerated away from the curb, the Bugatti disappearing into the night.

The night was dark and moonless, the only illumination coming from the paint glow of street lights that lined the highway. The air was heavy with the scent of wet asphalt and the distant hum of crickets provided a soothing background melody.

# CHAPTER 9
## The La Regina Della

My eyes flicked to the rear view mirror, my gaze locking on to the car tailing me. My Instincts kicked in, a surge of adrenaline coursing through my veins.

"*So soon ?*" I muttered to myself, a wry smile twisting my lips. With a Swift motion, I floored the Bugatti's engine roaring to life as I accelerated down the highway. The speedometer needle quivered, climbing higher and higher as I pushed the car to its limit.

The pursuing car struggled to keep up, its tires screeching in protest as it took the corners. My smile grew wider, my confidence in my driving skills unwavering.

But the pursuing car refused to give up, its headlights illuminating the dark Highway like a persistent shadow. My eyes darted between the road ahead and the rear view mirror, my mind racing with strategic possibilities.

I took a sharp turn, the bugatti's tyres hugging the curve as I accelerated out of the bend. The pursuing car followed suit, its driver seemingly determined to keep me in their sight. My grip on the steering wheel tightened, my knuckles whitening as I pushed the car to its limits. The speedometer needle quiverd at 120, 130, 140 miles per hour, the wind rushing passed the car like a vortex.

But no matter how fast I drove, the pursuing car remained hot on my heels. Its driver refused to back down. My eyes narrowed, my mind racing with a growing sense of unease.

My eyes snap to the horizon, my gaze looking on to the distant headlights. My heart sank, achil running down my spine. I was trapped. One car was telling me its driver was relentless in their pursuit. And now another car was waiting for me up ahead, its headlights casting an ominous glow on the dark highway.

My mind was racing, I quickly assessed my options. I could try to outrun the car behind me but the car ahead posed a significant obstacle. I could not try to swerve around it, but that would put me at risk of losing control.

Our cars were closing in, the distance between them shrinking with every passing second. My grip on the steering wheel tightened, my knuckles white with tension. I knew I had to think fast or risk being trapped. With a deep breath I made a split second decision.

I approached the car blocking my path, mere inches away from it, I made a split second decision with lightning quick reflexes, I yanked the steering wheel to the left taking a sharp detour onto the shoulder.

The car behind me, unable to react in time, slammed into the stationary vehicle with incredible force. The sound of crunching metal and scattering glass filled the air as the two cars collided. A massive fireball erupted engulfing both vehicles as they exploded on impact. The blast was so powerful that it sent a shock wave, rippling through the air, rockings my car as I sped away.

My eyes got a glimpse of the inferno in my rear view mirror. I felt a rush of adrenaline mixed with relief, knowing I'd narrowly escaped the deadly trap. With my heart still racing, I floored it, disappearing into the night.

I slowed down my car, my heart still racing from the close call. I pulled over to the side of the highway, putting the car in park. For a moment, I just sat there taking deep breaths to calm myself down. As I collected my thoughts, my eyes glanced in the rear view mirror again, half expecting to see another car following me. But the road behind me was empty, let only by the faint glow of the Moon.

Feeling a sense of relief was over me, I put the car in gear and continued driving. This time, I kept to a slow but normal speed, myself still on high alert. As I drove, I couldn't shake the feeling that I was being watched. Eyes glanced around, but the darkness seemed to swallow everything whole. My group on the steering wheel softened, my eyes scanning the road ahead.

My car spread along the highway, its headlights illuminating the dark asphalt. Above me a second highway loomed, its supports rising like giant pillars from the ground. The upper Highway crossed over the lower one at a perpendicular angle, forming a giant "T" shape that stretched across the landscape. As I drove, I glanced up at the underside of the upper highway, its concrete slab a blur above me.

As I was getting closer to the upper highway, I noticed a group of four standing on the roadside above me, on the upper highway. They were dressed in black suits, their faces obscured by the shadows. What caught my attention, however, was the guns clutched in their hands. The men's eyes seemed to be fixed on my car. Their gazes followed me as I drove by. My instincts screamed at me to get out of there, fast.

Yet I came closer to the upper highway, the four men started firing. The sound of gunfire Accord through the air as the man opened fire, their bullets whizzing post my car. I ducked instinctively, my heart racing. The rear windshield shattered, sending shards of glass flying everywhere. With a surge of adrenaline, I spun the wheel, making a sharp U-turn on the highway. My car's tires screeched in protest as I floored it, speeding away from the danger zone. In a maneuver, I made a complete circle on the road, narrowly avoiding the men's line of fire. As I completed the circle, I accelerated, my car shooting forward like a bullet. I didn't look back, instead, I kept my eyes fixed on the road ahead, my heart pounding in my chest.

As I glanced over my shoulder to see if the men were gone, my mind preoccupied with the gunmen. I didn't notice the truck barreling down on me from the right side of the road. The truck slammed into my car, sending it careening out of control. The impact sent my car spinning wildly, my world was turned upside down as my car spun wildly, my senses reeling from the impact. I immediately lost my consciousness.

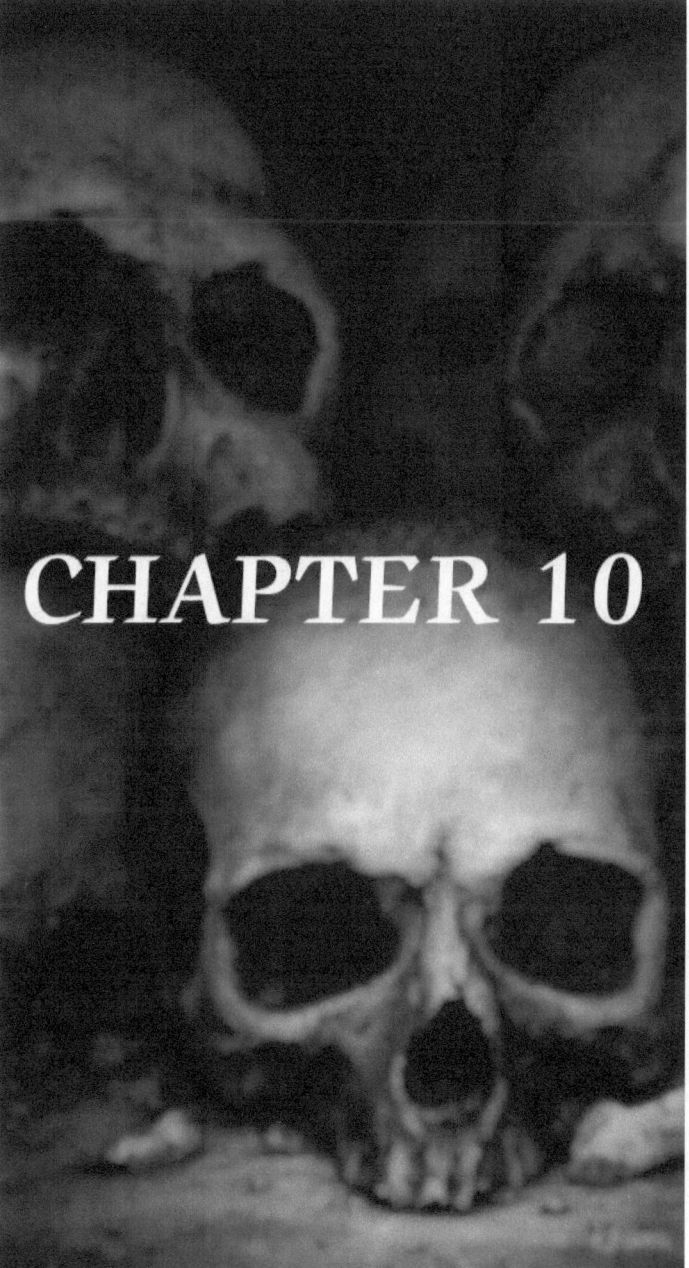

<u>I am Galentine Kriegal. I'm one of the rao. I belong form the Onaviirs part of the Road. I was given with a task to kidnap Adira, after her accident with the truck. After 15 minutes, I started my task, and reached to the destination, with my few teammates.</u>

15 minutes had passed since the crash, and Adira's car lay upside down, its mangled wreckage a testament to the force of the impact. Adira herself was half in, half out of the car. Her body limp and unconscious. A small pool of blood had formed on the ground beside her, a stark remainder of the severity of her injuries. The surrounding air was heavy with silence, punctuated only by the creeks and drones of the twisted metal.

Just as it seemed like Adira lay there forever, our sleek black car pulled up beside her. Me and one of my teammates stepped out, tall and imposing, with broad shoulders and chiseled features. We were dressed in black suits, our faces stern and unyielding. We stepped out, our faces obscured by the shadows. Without hesitation, we strode over to Adira's limp form and grasped her arms, dragging her away from the wreckage. We heaved her into the back seat of our car, flaming the door shut behind her. The engine roared to life, and our car sped away into the darkness, leaving behind the mangled remains of Adira's car and eerie silence of the road

# CHAPTER 11
## Rauf

# FEW HOURS LATER

I got to know about the accident, and I immediately informed Rivaan. We both left for the accident's spot.

The morning Sun cast its golden light upon the road, illuminating the scene of the previous night's accident. Rivaan, me, a few cops and Rivaan's gang members, stood at the spot where Adira's car had crashed, his eyes fixed on the Tangled wreckage. He pulled out his phone and dialed Zara's number. As she answered, Rivaan's voice was firm but controlled. He put the phone on speaker.

*"Where's Adira ?"*

*"I-I don't know...I haven't seen her."*

*"No need to lie, Zara. Adira met with an accident. I'm standing at the location right now."*

There was a pause on the other end of the line, followed by Zara's shocked gasp.

*"H-how did you....?"* She stammered.

Rivaan's jaw clenched in anger. He didn't give Zara a chance to finish her question. With a Swift motion, he hung up the call, his eyes blazed with anger as he processed the fact that Zara had tried to hide the truth from him. Why had they kept this from him ?

Soon, Zara arrived at the location. Zara's arrival was marked by the sound of screeching tires as such pulled up beside the wreckage. She stepped out of her car, her eyes fixed on the mangled remains of Adira's vehicle. As she stood beside Rivaan, her gaze fell upon the blood stains on the ground, and her eyes fixed, welled up the tears.

She took a deep breath, trying to compose herself, but her voice trembled as she began to murmur. *"I suggested her, she should tell you...but she denied...Lennox has her."*

Zara's words trailed off as she turned to Rivaan, her eyes pleading for reassurance. *"Do you think she is still alive ?"*

Rivaan's eyes narrowed as he gazed at Zara. *"They know who she belongs to, they would never dare to kill her."* he said, his voice low and even. Zara's eyes widened as she processed Rivaan's words.

Then a police officer, dressed in a crisp uniform, approached Rivaan. And he spoke in Russian. *"It seems that this is not an accident but some personal enmity. I'm afraid our hands are tied, Mr Rivaan."* His voice was apologetic. *"The agreement of 1927, you know, it's a binding contract that prohibits us from interfering in certain matters. Like it's your personal enmity. But we can try to...facilitate the process. However, it will require a significant amount of paperwork and...creative problem solving. And it will take...considerable time."*

Rivaan's eyes flashed with anger as he turned to the cop. *"Play a side role, as you always do...because of the...agreement of 1927."* Rivaan said mockingly, his voice dripping with sarcasm. The cop stood quiet. *"I don't have that...considerable time. I'll find her myself. You just make sure that you guys don't come in my way intentionally or unintentionally."*

The cop shifted uncomfortably, seeming to sense that Rivaan was not a man to be underestimated. Without another word, Rivaan turned and walked away, leaving the cops to exchange uneasy glances.

While Rivaan, me and Zara were walking back, Zara's eyes locked into Rivaan's. "*From where are you starting ?*" She asked Rivaan.

"*From burning the world.*" Rivaan's tone dripped with mockery that the task ahead was impossible, but he was willing to try anyway.

"*You're not Zade Meadows.*"

"*I can be, for her, I can be. As well as I can burn the world for her, at least I will try.*"

"*Well, I would like to see one example.*"

Rivaan's smirk grew, he then turned to me. "*I want the city on fire. I want Adira back.*"

"*Fire ?*"

"*Yeah, fire.*"

"*Oh that fire.*"

"*Yeah, that fire.*"

My tone dripped with understanding. It was clear that Rivaan's words were a code, a signal for something sinister. Zara wondered what exactly Rivaan had just set in motion.

"*What exactly do you mean ?*"

"*I won't find Adira myself. Lennox himself will send her to me.*"

# CHAPTER 12
## Galentine

*KAIRAOS BASE,* is the Central command centre and headquarters of Lennox's and Mastermind's operations. It serves as the nerve centre for strategic planning, surveillance, and mission control. It is located in a disclosed location, the facility is divided into various sections.

Deep within the vast Kairaos Base, Adira was being held captive in a surprisingly ordinary room. The space was simple, with plain white walls and a simple window that allowed a sliver of natural light to enter. A standard door, devoid of any ominous iron or reinforced plating, served as the only entry and exit point. The absence of jail type poles overt security measures belied the fact that Adira was, indeed, a prisoner. The room's unassuming appearance only added to the sense of unease and disorientation.

---

Lennox was so happy with my planning and execution to kidnap Adira. We decided to pay a visit to Adira. I reached her room, before anybody else.

Adira remained slumped forward in the wooden chair, unconscious and motionless, just as she had been since the previous night. Her body showed no signs of stirring, her chest rising and falling with slow, steady breaths. The silence in the room was oppressive, punctuated only by the occasional creek of the faint hum of the fluorescent lights overhead. Time seemed to steal as Adira lingered in her unconscious state, unaware of the passing hours or the fate that awaited her.

Adira's eyes snapped open as the sound of heavy footsteps echoed through the room, shattering The silence. She winced, her head pounding from the sudden noise. As her gaze cleared, she took in her surroundings, and her mind racing, she realised she was in the Kairaos Base. Her eyes widened as she saw Lennox, flanked by a few imposing Raos, stride into the room. Adira's body stiff from the long, uncomfortable night in the chair. Lennox's gaze locked on to hers, and he began to speak his voice low. "Welcome Adira."

As Adira's ears picked up the familiar timbre of Lennox's voice, her gaze snapped upward, locking onto his. She let out a dramatic sigh, rolling her eyes heavenward in exasperation. Lennox continued. "*You and your brother, you guys are so chaotic.*" His eyes reflected an expression of tiredness.

"*Chaos runs in our blood, Lennox.*" Adira replied, her voice low and husky, with a hint of pride and a dash of warning that sparkled in her eyes like a challenge. The words drift from her lips like Honey, sweet and tantalizing, yet laced with a subtle menaces. Lennox bent towards her and sneered. "*Adira, sweet captive...your brother's fear still lingers in this room. Soon, yours will join his.*"

"*You have unleashed hell, Lennox. (Eyes blazing) Rivaan will descend upon you like vengeance incarnate. My brother's kidnapping sealed your fate...and your screams will soon accompany my brother's.*"

"*You dare mock me with Rivaan's name ? I'll flay your brother before you, then crave Rivaan's heart out with his own dagger...and force-feed it to you ! Your lover's deadly reputation only amuse me."*

*"Amuse ? You tremble inside, Lennox. My love will reduce you to ashes. Ashes infused with your own screams. Rivaan will make your agony legendary...and I'll whisper his name in your ear as darkness claims you."*

*"(Spittle flying) Legendary agony ?! You think Rivaan's fearsome rumours can touch me ?! I've bathed in blood, Adira - innocent and guilty alike. Your brother's life force is still warming my hands...proves my dominion."*

*"(Unfazed) Dominion of cowards. Rivaan has faced true darkness, and emerged stronger. His blade has tasted the evil you worship...and he'll serve you the same fate. Rivaan carves your twisted soul from its rott."*

*"Wait...Is that a warning ?"*

*"Did it sound like a compliment ?!"*

*"No, no. But if Rivaan...that arrogant fool thinks he can save you, I'll hang his corpse beside you and your brother's!"*

*"Maybe you'll be the one hanging...from Rivaan's hand, begging for death. My love always claims what's his."*

Lennox's anger boiled. He punched Adira, her head snapping sideways from the impact. She clenched her jaw, wincing briefly before sitting straight again, a chilling smirk spreading across her face. Her voice laced with disdain. *"That's it ? Is this all you have, the strength for a single punch ? This is what you can muster...hiding behind walls and bodyguards ? Why bother, Lennox ? So that I don't rise from this chair...and behead you, and spill your entrails on this floor ?"*

Lennox's face darkness, fury shimmering. He again bends towards Adira, gripped the top backrest of her chair tightly and said in a low, menacing tone. *"Should I show you my strength, my stamina ? As a man* ( he looked at her lips) *I can do a lot more. As a man...I'll demonstrate men's power...beyond love. Rivaan may have your heart.* (He leaned closer, his lips brushing her ears) *But I'll break your spirit. I'll have your body.* ( Hot breath dancing upon her skin) *You've mocked my strength...time will come soon...when I'll demonstrate what a real man can do to a defiant little girl like you."*

Adira's eyes locked into Lennox's, fear bleeding into her gaze like ink on wet paper. Her defiance dissolves, replaced by a chilling vulnerability. For an instant, she's frozen, transfixed by Lennox's menacing stare. Then, her pupils dilate further, fear deepening...a faint tremble dances across her battered lips. Lennox's grip on her chair tightens, as if sending victory over her spirit.

Lennox stood tall, his voice cold and commanding. *"Hit her until she begs you to stop."* Lennox's eyes gleaming with cruelty as he watches his men move into position. The two Raos quickly bind Adira's right hand to the armrest with handcuffs. Adira's left hand remains free. Then one rao threw a vicious punch to her face, Adira's head jerked sideways. He follows with a blow belly she doubles over slightly, gasping and that one single pinch on belly was so strong that it made Adira to split blood. Then, rapid fire punches land on her face.

**One** punch splits her lips.

**Two** bruises on her cheekbone.

**Three** swells her eye socket.

**Four** cracks her jaw.

**Five** leaves her gasping....Adira's battered face slumps forward slightly as they paused. Adira's head reels, face bloody and battered. Her black coat hangs open, revealing the devastating aftermath. Her black silk loose top beneath was drenched, soaked through with her own blood. The fabric clings to her torso, stained crimson from neck to waist. Blood drops slowly from her chin, falling onto the silk like morbid raindrops.

The brutality resumes. Punch **SIX** cracks her already swollen eye socket further. **SEVEN, EIGHT, NINE–––SEVENTEEN.**

Adira's swift movement saved her from further brutality. She placed her left hand gently, before her injured face, her palm facing outward. She finally put her hand up to stop us. A desperate gesture pleading for mercy. Her body tense with anticipation. She closed her eyes, bracing for impact. expecting the Rao's fist to still crashdown, crushing her face further. Her eyelids squeeze shut, tears leaking from the corners. Bloodshot right eye now hidden from sight.

Swollen right eye already closed but she tightens her face muscle anyway, preparing for agony. Her chest rises slightly, ahead breath waiting for the punch that may still come...dead silence from Lennox and the Rao's. Adira's help breath escaped in a sharp gasp as she realized that we had stopped. Her eyes snap open. She blinks slowly, taking in the scene. Lennox standing tall, observing her intensely. The room silent, except for her own ragged breathing.

Adira's groan fills the air, a raw expression of pain and defiance. Then, her voice explodes- *"Fuck !!"* Echoes of her furious shout lingar before she clears her throat, as if scraping away vulnerability. Her poster transformed instantly. She sat straight, shoulder squared, despite obvious agony. Her spine stiffens, defiance palpable as she talks a deep, deliberate breath, just rising slowly, painfully.

Adira's intense gaze at Lennox flatters, replaced by a sudden spark of recollection. Her eyes widen slightly, as if a hidden door in her mind swung open. Her hand instinctively dips into the front pocket of her Black jeans, fingers closing around a familiar shape. She pulls out a cigarette, slender fingers grasping it tightly, a habitual comfort sought amidst turmoil.

The cigarette found its way to her lips, poised between them. Adira gestures lazily to the guard, cigarette still clamped between her lips. A silent command for a lighter. The guard's eyes flick instantly to Lennox, seeking permission. Lennox's gaze remained fixed on Adira, then he nodded almost imperceptibly, a vertical head motion: up, down - approval granted.

The Rao understood, pulled out a lighter from his pocket, and walked slowly towards Adira. His hand still smeared with Adira's dried blood. Fumbles for the lighter, flip it open, and Sparks a flame. Adira leans into the bloody hand, cigarette tip glowing Orange as flames kiss it.

Serenity in suffering.

Adira inhales deeply, cigarette smoke feeling her lungs. Her eyes drift closed, eyelets relaxing like heavy curtains. Her head tilts backward, Chin pointing towards the ceiling as if surrendering to momentary bliss. The room's tense atmosphere seems to fade from her awareness briefly. Then, slowly exhaling. Her head begins a circular motion, rolling gently clockwise. Chin to right shoulder, back towards ceiling, left shoulder, returning to centre. Smoke curls lazily from her lips, entwining with her hypnotic head movement. Eyes still closed, peaceful expression... until her head stopped moving.

Adira's eyes snap open, locking onto Lennox's intense gaze. A sly smile spreads across her bettered face, swollen lips curling upwards. Lennox's expression twists in anger, his voice low and menacing. *"This bitchcraft won't have any effect on me."*

Adira's smile widened slightly as she chuckled softly, a husky laugh that sent shivers down Lennox's spine. Her voice dripped with amusement. *"Oh really ? But I think it's already having..."*

Lennox's eyes narrowed, jaw clenched. Lennox spined towards his Rao, voice cracking with frustration and anger. His words tumbling out in a stammering rage.*"W-What...happened to her ?! Why is she, smiling like that ?! Where's all her pain ?! A minute ago she was...she was Groaning in agony !"* His face purples, with Fury, veins bulging as he gestures wildly towards Adira. Her calm demeanor and sly smile seem to enrage him further.

Lennox's eyes widened as I started explaining. *"Sir, that cigarette...it has a black and golden line on the filter. I've seen that mark before, it's a specially designed cigarette, filled with the powerful drug codenamed '**Kryptonite steel**'... It alters nerve receptors, making her body akin to metal.*

*Numbs pain receptors completely. She'll feel no agony now. At least as long as the effect remains in her system...sir, intel suggests 3-4 hours before it wears off."*

Lennox's face twists in outrage and fascination. He turns slowly back to Adira, eyes burning with intensity. Adira smirks slightly, confirming my words. Her swollen eyes seem almost...comfortable now. Her pain free demeanor only seems to intensify his interrogation desire. Lennox was about to say something when suddenly his phone rang. He checked the caller ID and exited the room. Where Adira was imprisoned. *"Come out."* He instructed. We nodded, returned to our posts outside, closed the door of her room softly behind us, leaving Adira alone once more.

# CHAPTER 13
*Rauf*

# 3 DAYS PASSED

Chaos erupts in Moscow streets. Rivaan's heavily armed men, clad in black bulletproof vest and helmets, wreak havoc:

- Machine guns blaze with precision fire power, cutting down civilians randomly.

- Grenades shatter windows, sending glass remaining on two side walls.

- Cars and vehicles erupt in flames, black smoke billowing into the air

- Screams of terrorized citizens pierce the din of destruction.

- Buildings' facades crater from rocket-propelled grenades.

- Rivaan's men move methodically, room by room, floor by floor.

Executing indiscriminate Carnage in offices, shops and restaurants. Moscow's streets resemble a war zone. Sirens wail in the distance. Police forces rush into Moscow streets, siren blaring. But they are grossly outmatched by Rivaan's heavily armed militants.

- Police cars are rammed, overturned, or riddled with bullets.

- Officers fall clutching wounds, others flee in panic.

- Tear gas developed by police is countered with militants' gas masks.

- SWAT teams engage, but Rivaan's men wield superior firepower, cutting down elite officers with precious shots.

- A police helicopter hovers above, but militants launch a missile, blasting the chopper from the sky in a fiery explosion. The Moscow police chief's desperate voice cracks on the radio. *"we are losing control..."* casualty numbers scroll on a nearby TV screen: *"police fertilities: 127. Civilians killed:124. Injured: over 500..."*

Amidst Moscow's blazing ruins and shattered glass, one building stands eerily intact, unscatted by Rivaan's chaos: his own sleek.

Windows gleaming, walls pristine, entrance untouched. No flames lick its exterior, no bullets car its facade. A deliberate exemption from the devastation surrounding it.

Rivaan's symbol-a Black snake. Remains polished on the entrance. Gleaming with ironic tranquility. The nearby streets resemble war zones, but his building stands. A haunting monument to Rivaan's calculator power and control.

Modern office in Moscow- a towering skyscraper. Inside it, a handsome figure sits behind a massive glass desk. His hair perfectly style, dark suit impeccable. Every inch the powerful Russian mafia.

Rivaan stood tall behind his office window, gaze fixed outward. Moscow burns and smalders under his relentless assault. A cigarette dangles from his lips, smoke curling lazily upwards. As he watches Chaos consume the city, he once called home. His eyes gleam with intensity, yet his expression remains calm. A contrast to the inferno raging below. I (Rauf) was standing in his office with him, looking at the destruction. That was the fire he wanted me to set Moscow on.

Then suddenly, a bunch of ministers burst into Rivaan's office. Faces red with rage. *"Enough of your dramas, Rivaan !"* the main thundered. Rivaan turned calmly from the window view of Moscow's chaos. He transferred the cigarette to an ashtray. And sliped his hands into his pockets. He came in front of his desk and stood there, leaning back at the desk a little. He faced the minister, expression serene.

*"This madness has lasted 3 days !"* Another minister spits. *"We've lost count of the dead...and for what ? Your twisted obsession with Adira !"*

Rivaan's eyes widened slightly, feigning surprise-*"Oh this ?"* he gestures to the Chaos outside. *"Yeah, I take the credit for this."*

One of the ministers smirks cynically-*"I think you mean 'blame'."* But the main minister, President Viktorov raises a hand, silencing the speaking minister. His expression turns polite, probing: *"Rivaan, tell me...is this devastation truly for Adira ? You love her, don't you ?"*

Rivaan's surprise faded, replaced by dry amusement; he leaned back slightly, voice low and candid. *"Was it that obvious ?"* No defiance, no denial, only acknowledgement. Viktorov's eyes narrowed. *"I didn't think you were the type to lose sanity over a woman."* he paused, studying Rivaan's calm demeanor, expecting a hint of emotion, but found none. Rivaan's response was immediate and chillingly candid. *"I didn't either."*

Their eyes lock in a silent understanding. Rivaan's eyes glint with amusement- *"Well, I think you guys forget the agreement of 1927."*

Minister Petrov's face turned red with outrage- *"That treaty was made for peace between the mafia and the government, not destruction of public property!"*

Rivaan chuckles low in his throat. *"Heaven! I am not even just destroying public property...I am simply destroying public... and property."*

The room falls silent, the ministers stunned by Rivaan's sinister wordplay. Then Viktorov asks nervously, *"what do you want, Rivaan, to stop this devastation?"* Expecting that he would ask something big.

Rivaan's gaze pierced through the tense-filled room- *"Krish...and especially Adira."* Ministers exchange stunned glances-*"Huh?! But what about the agreement of 1927?"* Minister Viktorov blurts out in disbelief. Rivaan calmly placed his cigarette back between his lips and came close to minister Viktorov. Minister. Viktorov, leaned in slightly, unaware of impending intimidation. Rivaan then inhaled slowly, the exhaled smoke directly at Viktorov's face, his voice low, menacing, and deliberate: *"I. Want. My. Adira & Krish. Back."* Smoke wafts across Petrov's, Viktorov's stunned expression as Rivaan continues- *"Or shall I...burn The Moscow...to ashes? It even falls under my area."* The room freezed, awaiting Viktorov's terrified response. Rivaan turned and walked towards his desk. *"Sir. I want you to deliver this message to Lennox precisely as spoken. Rivaan demands Krish & Adira's immediate return to his Moscow headquarters, Raven hurst. Their presence is required to cease current...rearrangements. Further devastation will escalate exponentially if compliance fails. Global Chaos Hinges on his corporation. Rivaan awaits Adira's return. Compliance expected."*

Minister Petrov finds voice first, outrage palpable. *"You're blackmailing us over a woman, Rivaan ?! Madness !"* Then minister Viktorov adds, tone laced with disgust- *"Adira's merely leverage for your twisted games, not worth the city's destruction."*

Rivaan blows out smoke slowly, unfazed by their outrage- *"Merely leverage ?"* He repeats Minister Viktorov's words, voice low and deadly- *"Adira belongs to me. She's mine. And you'd do well to remember, I always collect what's mine."*

Minister Viktorov scoffs- *"Lennox will never hand her over !"* Rivaan smiled- *"Unwise. Lennox's refusal would be...unwise."*

The room hangs in heavy silence. Ministers exchange nervous glances, wanting to speak but frozen. Rivaan breaks The silence, his voice firm- *"Enough contemplation, ministers. My patience expires. Leave."*

Ministers rapidly composed themselves, nodding collectively. The file out of the room with urgency, doors closing behind them. Silence reigns once more.

Then, Rivaan turned to me and asked. *"Can I hit them all with a knife, just a little bit ?"*

*"I believe the technical term is 'stab'."* I replied.

# CHAPTER 14
## The La Regina Della

# IN KAIRAOS BASE

I wasn't healing much. But I couldn't wait to get recovered and then attempt to run. But I was better than I was 3 days ago. So I decided to run away. It would not make much difference for my future, if you know what I mean.

I slowly slide my legs under my chair, stretching to reach my bounded hands. Behind my back, tied to the chair's frame. A hidden compartment clicks open, revealing a thin blade from my shoes. I grasped the blade between my fingers, maneuvering it carefully, starting to see through the durable ropes binding my wrists. The blade glides smoothly, cutting fibres with precision, ropes frays, loosen...

My eyes widened slightly at the unexpected interruption. A woman burst into my room, chainsaw roaring to life in her hands. "*Tryna run sis ? Lemme help you !*" the woman said with sarcasm. My sense trap, her tone doesn't match helpful intent. I silently free my hands from ropes. Then swiftly grab the back rest of my chair, my grip firm.

Then that woman suddenly charged towards me, chainsawed, held high- unaware of my newly gained freedom and prepared a counter attack. I swang my chair forward with powerful precision. Chair crashes into the woman, momentarily stunning her, hitting her squarely across the torso. The woman grunts, stunned, and chainsaw flies from her hand. She stumbles backward, momentarily dazed from chair impact. I prepared for combat. The woman dives toward the chains on the floor, hands grasping for handles. I anticipated the woman's moves, I jumped forward, elbow striking down like a dagger, then the woman's neck met my elbow, a temporary chokehold applied.

The woman's eyes widened, gasping - chainsaw, eyes locked on me. Fist clenched, she charges towards her enemy, me. I stood ready, hands up in guard position. The woman unleashes a flurry of punches. I blocked or dodged most. A few strikes slip through, glancing off my draw and shoulder. I counter attack with precise kicks and elbows. The woman absorbed blows, relentless in her assault. The battle rages on, punches fly, bodies clash. I mostly defended, saving myself from the woman's fierce offence. I landed occasional solid hits, but the woman's fierce offense.

Driving by rage or adrenaline, the woman seemed barely phased. Suddenly I saw an opening, the woman leaves neck exposed. But before I act the woman pushed me toward the wall, and grabbed the chainsaw again.

My back pressed against the cold room wall. I stood frozen, ice fixed on the woman's snarling face. The woman's chains of roars menacingly, mere inches from my face. My hands grasped the woman's wrist and forearms, struggling to restrain the chainsaw's deadly bite, muscle trembling.

Sweat drips down my face as I lean backward trying to increase the distance between my skin and whirring teeth. The women's eyes blaze with fury.

The woman's grip became weak, she got tired. I seize the opportunity, I shove the woman backwards. The woman lost balance, arms failing. I pushed the chainsaw towards her. The woman's hand instinctively grabs chainsaw's handle, unaware of danger. Then I hit on the woman's hand and grabbed her hand, and pushed her hands toward her face, due to which, the chains of blade bite into the woman's face. A vertical gas from forehead to chain. A 105° cut, deep but not fully dissecting. Upper layers of skin and flash torn open, bleeding profusely. The woman's eyes widened in horror, she tried to pull chains away but she just couldn't. The Blade remains lodged in her face, skin pinched around metal.

The woman's screams echo- mixture of pain, shock and terror. I stumbled back, my eyes fixed on the woman's gruesome injury. I stood tall, still processing the intense battle aftermath. I took slow, deep breaths, calming nerves and clearing mind. I was injured too, and now tired. Then, my hand reached for my pocket. Producing a cigarette. I then picked up the lighter which fell on the floor from the woman's pocket. I lit up, inhaled deeply the nicotine coursing through veins, Momentarily numbing emotional and physical pain.

Exhaling the smoke slowly, I felt a slight calm descent. Enough to focus on escape and next moves. I eye the woman's prone form. Then turns away, resolved. Picks up the silent bloodied chainsaw, grip firm in hand. I step out of my room into the corridor, hallways stretch both directions, alarms sirens begin wailing.

I leaned against the corridor wall, eyeing newcomers. Irritation flashes across my face- *"seriously ? Bruh..."*

I muttered to myself and rolled eyes. I took a long drag on my cigarette, exhaling slowly. Smoke curls around my head as I gazed at the men in front of me. Axes and knives glinted in fluorescent lighting (They were the Kamikazes) my expression turned mocking. I flicked cigarette ash towards them. With the laze gesture, I beckons attackers closer. Palm unturned, fingerings curling inward, a sarcastic, *"come hither."* Motion. The man exchanged glances, axes and knives gripped tighter. Then, with battle reise, they charged towards me, chainsaw at ready.

15 minutes had passed, I had already killed most of them. I was attacking everyone wildly. I was all drenched in blood. I grabbed the neck of one kamikaze. My grip closes around his neck. I lifted him off the ground, his feet kicking wildly. Slams his body against the corridor wall, aligning his neck with a rusty window edge. The half open window's sharp, corroded metal glint menacingly. My Palm presses his

neck against the window frame, leveraging my strength. With sudden force, I slammed the window shut- metal bites deep into his flash. The kamikaze's body goes limp-head partially severed, dangling gruesomely. I released the grip, letting the corpse collapse to the ground.

Then I turned to the remaining Kamikazes, expressing unchanging. I took a slow drag on the cigarette, exhaling smoke calmly. Eyes narrowing slightly. I seemed to savor their terror. I drop cigarette, grinding into the floor with my boot. With chainsaw still in hand, I advanced towards the survivors.

Their axes and knives tremble as they back away slowly. One step forward, swing the axe wildly. I smetes faintly. He came running to me, and attacked. I dodged axe swings by mere inches. Counter attacks with chainsaw, slicing through attackers thigh. He collapses screaming, clutching wounded leg. I straddle his torso, sitting firmly before his abdomen. Pinning him down with my weight, immobilizing his upper body.

With chilling precision, I revs chainsaw. Placed the blade tip on his zygoma (*a bone that forms the cheek and part of the eye socket)* and then pressed it downward. Chainsaw bites through skin, muscle, and bone with gruesome ease. Dissecting his face vertically from the zygoma to the opposite zygoma, splitting the front face *(including frontal region, eye, lips, nose and cheeks)* and the rear face *(including ears, and head, here)*

The person's screams cease, replaced by blood-choked gurgles. I continued the chainsaw till it dissected and touched the floor. I then shuts off the chainsaw, rises from the corpse. Chest heaving slightly from exertion, eyes gleaming with intensity. Only one kamikaze left, he too ran away. I then stood up, and picked up the sunglasses drenched in blood, they were laying on the floor. And I wore it and started walking.

My legs buckled suddenly. I crashed to the corridor floor and became unconscious.

# CHAPTER 15
## Galentine

Me and Lennox watched footage of Adira's rampage on the monitor screens. Her unconscious body lay still, surrounded by Carnage she created. Our eyes widened in surprise, then narrowed in begrudging respect. *"Damn...she's more formidable that I gave her credit for."* Lennox leaned back in chair, steepling fingers together. A calculating glint appears in his eyes. *"Call Rivaan...I can't afford to keep her here."* Lennox smirks, anticipating Rivaan's confidence, *"But we should first give him a surprise."* I nodded, *"Calling Rivaan now, sir. Patching through..."*

Rivaan's voice came on line. Lennox said into the phone, *"Rivaan, Krish awaits extraction at Vladivostok port. Send your team...he'll be...cooperative."* Lennox added with a hint of sly tone- *"And Adira will arrive soon as well."* Rivaan's silence on line was palpable. Lennox imagined his intense gaze.

# RAUF AS NARRATOR

Rivaan, me(Rauf), Zara and some of Eves and Rivaan's gang members, reached Vladivostok port, with a chaotic sound of cars. Rivaan stepped out of his Syrah color Rolls Royce, La Rosa Naire. Droptail onto Vladivostok port. His eyes scanned the surroundings before focusing upward. A crane Tower looms, it's hook suspending a body high above, Krish's lifeless form hangs eerily still, swaying gently in the breeze. Krish's face was brutally stabbed, knife wounds gaping open. Stomach cavity ripped open, organs bulging out like gruesome balloons, intestine, stomach lining, and liver hang loosely, swaying with each gentle breeze.

Skin torn, flesh hanging loose like macabre ribbons. Pieces of cheek and forehead dangling precariously, barely attached. Rivaan's eyes widened in shock. His vision blurs momentarily. Then his gaze shifts a little more upward. Krish's head a nightmare scenario. Right Half of skull missing, brain exposed, dangling by fragile tissue.

Eye socket empty, jawbone cracked, teeth visible. A macabre grimace frozen on remaining facial skin. Rivaan's leg buckled, he collapsed to knees, hands grasping port ground. Dry leaves rack his body as mind struggles. This wasn't the first time he saw something like this, but he never wanted it to be Krish.

Rivaan's eyes locked into Krish's remains. Fueling unrelenting fury and vow of devastating revenge against Lennox.

Rivaan's strong facade crumbles in shock and grief etch his face. Tears well up his eyes, blurring vision of Krish's lifeless body. He felt like he'd been punched in the gut, wind knocked out of him. His mind reels with devastating thoughts. *"I had promised to Adira...and...I failed ? I-I failed."* He murmured.

Rivaan's eyes drop, fixating on the ground as tears fall. He whispered barely audibly -*"What do I tell Adira...Krish was her only family left...How can I let this happen?"* Thoughts of Adira's impending arrival haunt him. *How will he break this news to her ? Will she ever forgive him for giving her a fake hope ? Is It all over now ?*

On the other hand, Zara was unconscious ath the first sight of Krish's body and lying on the ground. I was looking at the body too. Suddenly Rivaan's phone rang, I had his phone, so I checked the caller's name. And hesitated to hand it over to Rivaan. *"Ri- Rivaan."* Rivaan looked straight at me.*"I don't wanna talk right now."* He said in a menacing tone. *"But it's Lennox."* I replied.

Rivaan's eyes filled with rage, and took the phone and his own hands. Lennox's laughter echoed through the phone speaker. Rivaan's grip tightened, fury barely contained. Lennox chuckles longer. Rivaan said. *"You'll pay for this. Witness her wrath, and mine. Krish was her family. I will be your destruction."*

*"Oh god...gotcha. That...decoration at Vladivostok port wasn't Krish."*

Rivaan took a breath of relief, and sighed heavily. *"But...your fate is written now."*

*"Well, well, we'll see 'bout that. For now...Krish is safe...for now. But Adira...your precious Adira...lies unconscious in mortuary section 3, St. Petersburg General Hospital and remember, my people are on their way to do her postmortem.*

*And her cell is filled with a...human liquid, so of course she might not be able to breathe unless she's a mermaid, HaHaHa* (stupid laugh) *Now, hurry up...otherwise don't say to minister Viktorov, that I didn't tell you before-"*

Rivaan's eyes widen, he commits location to memory instantly. Hospital name and Maurya section etched in the brain like a battle plan. He'll move swiftly, extracting Adira before Lennox orchestrates further chaos. Lennox added lazily- *"visit her soon, Rivaan. My...gift to her requires your prompt attention."* phone call ends. Rivaan springs into action, we both sat in his car, and all the cars just disappear in a few seconds. Real soon he reached to the St. Petersburg hospital.

Rivaan burst into mortuary section 3. He rushed to the locker number given by Lennox. Grabs handle, twists, and pulls, metal cracks open. Suddenly a blood Dam breaks. A torrent of cold, crimson liquid bursts out, flooding floor.

Rivaan leaks back, blood pours out like a macabre waterfall, pooling around his feet. As blood flows slow, revealing the locker's interior. Adira's pale face comes into view, unconscious body submerged. Her skin deathly white, lips bluish. Rivaan's heart sank, he rushed forward, wading through blood. Gently lifts Adira out of the locker, cradling her in arms. Her head lolls back, mouth slightly open. He checked pulse- weak but present. Rivaan exhales deeply, relief mixed with rage towards Lennox. He looks at Adira over multiple wounds, bruises, and stitches. Lennox's *'gift'* - evidence of Adira's brutal fight for survival.

Soft morning sunlight streams through the wall sized window. Rivaan had brought her with him, in his mansion. She was still unconscious. The morning sunlight illuminates Adira's peaceful face, casting gentle glow on her skin. White gown draped gently around her bandaged body. Oxygen mask covers her nose and mouth, whooshing sound a company each breath. Doctors and nurses move quietly around her beside. Monitoring equipment beeps softly, tracking vital signs. IV drips feed medication into her veins, aiding recovery. Rivaan stands frozen in the doorway, eyes fixed intensely. Drinking in every detail of Adira's vulnerable state. His expression complex, concern, relief and fierce protectiveness entwined.

He leans against the door frame, arms crossed over chest. Watching her chest rise and fall with each slow breath. Assurance that she still lives, still fights. One doctor notices Rivaan, approaches him softly. *"Meds are helping, she'll awake soon."* Rivaan nods softly, never leaving Adira's face. *"keep me updated. Any change...anything, inform me immediately."*

Doctor nodes, returns to monitoring Adira's progress. Rivaan remains vigilant in doorway, guarding her rest. After all the doctors left, Rivaan came and sat gently on the bed beside Adira. His fingers brushing softly against her cheeks, forehead, and hair. Eyes overflowing with love, concern and relief.

Just then, a soft knock at the door. Rivaan's guard, Vikram, enters- *"sir Zara requests audience with Ms. Adira."* Rivaan shaked his head to allow. Then Zara came and sat beside Adira, opposite side of Rivaan. Her eyes looking onto Adira's face. Tears well up instantly, brimming over as she gazes at Adira's bandaged form. Rivaan stood, arms folded, watching Adira and Zara. *"Why is she here ?"* Zara asked.

Rivaan's eyes narrowing slightly. Expression turns glacial. Yet she continues, voice above whisper. *"she should be at home...with us. It's not her home."*

*" We need to talk outside 'bout this."* Rivaan gestures firmly towards the door. Zara rises from bed, tears still falling. Zara follows Rivaan out of the room, closing the door behind them.

# CHAPTER 16
## Zara

Me (Zara) and Rivaan, just as we exited Adira's room, Rivaan pulled out a cigarette and lit it. Burning tobacco filling the air as he stepped into the hallway confrontation with me. The intense conversation unfolds like a volatile dance. Me and Rivaan exchange biting words, each step escalating tension.

"*Yes. So tell, what were you saying inside?*" Rivaan asked, his voice low and dangerous. A shiver ran down my spine. The air crackled between us, thick with unspoken tension. I hated this. Hated how he could make my heart pound and my anger simmer all at once.

"*This is your home. Not her's.*" I said, my voice firm despite the tremor in my hands. I clenched them into fists at my sides. Stay strong, Zara. Don't let him intimidate you.

"*She's also mine.*" His eyes, those intense golden eyes, locked onto mine. I felt a surge of possessiveness in his tone that both terrified and...something else. Something I refused to acknowledge.

"*No, Rivaan.*" I insisted, trying to keep my voice even. He can't claim her like this. It's not right.

*"Yes, Zara."* He stepped closer, invading my personal space. I had to tilt my head back to meet his gaze. It was a battle of wills, and I was determined not to be the first to break.

*"No, Rivaan. That's not how it works."* My breath hitched. He was too close. Too overwhelming.

*"That's exactly how it works."* A hint of a smirk played on his lips. He knew he was getting to me. I could feel my control slipping.

*"No. It doesn't."* I repeated, my voice barely a whisper. Don't let him see your weakness.

*"Then I'll make it work."* Rivaan never wants to back down. He thrived on confrontation, on pushing boundaries. It was one of the many things that made him so infuriating. And so...compelling. I pushed that thought away. Focus, Zara.

*"Rivaan. She needs us. She needs her own people."* I pleaded, trying a different tactic. Appealing to his sense of reason, though I knew it was a long shot.

*"Her own people ? What do you mean by her 'own people' ? Who the fuck am I to her, then ?"* He exploded, his voice laced with fury and a hint of something that sounded

almost like pain. It caught me off guard. He actually cares. More than he should.

*"I don't know. But you cannot keep her with you."* I said, my voice softer now. I could feel my resolve wavering. He was tearing down my defenses brick by brick.

*"Oh dear, I can."* His eyes glittered with a dangerous possessiveness. It was a declaration of war.

*"You are not her husband."* I reminded him, stating the obvious, clinging to any semblance of logic.

*"I will be."* He said it with such certainty, such conviction, it sent a fresh wave of unease through me. He's serious. This is more than just a power play.

*"Talk about right now. No right to keep her with you or care for her."* I pressed on, trying to ignore the way my stomach was twisting itself into knots.

*"She. Belongs. To. Me. I don't need fucking rights."* He punctuated each word with a step closer, until I could feel his breath on my face. The sheer force of his will was a tangible thing, pressing down on me.

*"What about permission, then ? Who gave you permission ?"* I challenged, my voice rising in defiance. I wouldn't back down. Not now.

*"Do I need permission?"* He scoffed, a dark amusement in his eyes.

*"Yes, you do."* I insisted, my heart pounding in my chest.

*"Heaven! Whose permission?"* He said the word *"Heaven"* with a wry twist, a flicker of surprise and something almost like a chuckle in his voice. It threw me for a moment. He's actually finding this...funny?

*"Hers."* I said, my voice firm.

*"She is unconscious."* He stated the obvious, his gaze unwavering.

*"You cannot take care of her, she's a woman, and she needs a woman."* I argued, my voice laced with desperation now. I was losing ground, and I knew it.

*"I can. And I will."* He growled, the possessiveness in his voice bordering on feral.

*"I am not stealing her."* I tried to convince, my voice pleading. Why won't he understand?

*"As if you can."* He sneered, his eyes mocking me.

*"Rivaan, please...don't separate her from us."* My voice cracked. I hated how vulnerable I sounded.

*"I am not separating, you can all live here."* He offered, but it wasn't a compromise. It was a command.

*"You are so stubborn, Rivaan."* I got irritated. My carefully constructed composure finally shattered.

*"Aren't you?"* He countered, his lips curling into a knowing smirk. He knew exactly how to push my buttons.

*"Enough, Rivaan. I'm taking Adira home with me."* I declared, my voice trembling with a mixture of anger and fear. I was done arguing. I was done trying to reason with him. I was taking her, no matter what

Rivaan looked at me. His gaze pierced my soul. His eyes transform into those of predators, intense and unyielding. His hunter eyes bored into mine, as if sizing up prey. He exhales slowly, cigarette smoke curling out his mouth. A languid stream of gray mist that dances between them. As if symbolizing the fragile thread of tension connecting our stares. My eyes widened slightly, pupils dilated, I seemed entrenched by Rivaan's hypnotic gaze, frozen in place. I instantly felt like I had said something I wasn't supposed to. His cigarette smoke wafts closer, carrying the scent of burning tobacco. Rivaan took a deliberate step closer, eyes burning bright. Trapping me in his intense stare. "*Take her...and you'll witness what my worst enemies do.*" His eyes gleamed with challenge, daring me to back down. The air thickened with tension as his words hang like a gauntlet thrown. My face sets in determination, a flicker of fear danced in my eyes. I knew Rivaan was not making idle threats, he'll fight fiercely for Adira. Cigarette still clutched between fingers, smoke curling lazily upwards. The silence between us became a living thing. "*Fine.*" I shouted in anger, "*but I'll keep checking on her, even in the middle of the night.*"

"*No problem.*" Then I turned and walked away leaving Rivaan standing in the hallway. His cigarette smoke curled lazily upwards as he watched me depart.

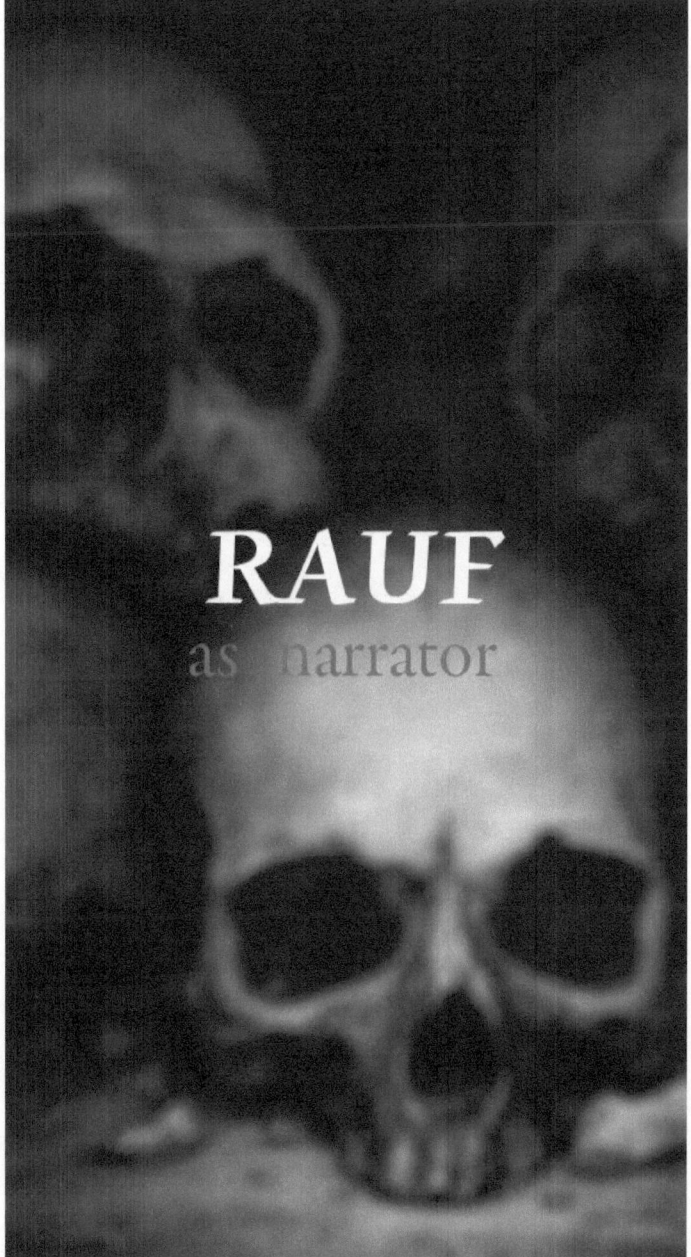

After Zara left, I came to Rivaan. And told him, "*she is conscious.*" Rivaan's eyes widened in excitement and relief exploding across his face. He crushed his cigarette into the nearby ashtery and rushed towards Adira's room. Feet pounding softly on plush carpet as he hurried to her side. Throws open door, and suddenly freezes. Transfixed by Adira's battered yet beautiful face. Adira sat half declined against pillows, nurse beside her. Returning water glass to tray, oblivious to Rivaan entrance.

# CHAPTER 17

## The La Regina Della

My gaze locked into Rivaan's, and my expression crumbled. Bruises, bandages, and swollen eye can't hide selling tears. My lower lip trembles, chin quivers. Sobs erupt like a dam breaking, body shakings violently. Rivaan Frozen state shattered, he rushed closer, dropping knees beside bed. "*Adira...*" his voice cracks with emotion, hands reaching tentatively. As if seeking to touch my injured face, my fragile soul. My crying intensified, tears streaming down my cheeks.

I buried my face in Rivaan's chest. His arms envelop me tightly, holding me close as tears soak his shirt. The room empties silently, nurses and guards slip out, granting privacy.

My muffled voice asked between sobs, "*Please tell me it was worth...Krish is back home...*" I felt Rivaan's chest rise with deep breath. He chose words carefully, avoiding the truth from me, "*You're so brave, Ad...we all including Krish, are so proud of you.*"

I pulled back slightly, eyes red rimmed. Hope and longing etched on my face as I asked. "*Where's Krish?*" Rivaan's gaze locked into mine. A hint of sadness flickered, quickly masked by a gentle smile. "*He's safe...*" My eyes narrowed faintly. Uncertainty creeps in, but exhaustion and pain prevail. I leaned back into Rivaan's chest, voice barely audible. *"Promise me...Krish is really safe."* Rivaan's embrace tightened. A safe whisper -*"I promise."* But his eyes betray turmoil heavy with unspoken sorrow.

---

# AT NIGHT

Moonlight streaming through open curtains illuminated my restless form. My eyes fluttered close only to snap back open, sleep elusive.

Rivaan leaned against the doorway, observing my turmoil. His presence silent until he spoke low and gentle. *"What happened, Ad ?"*

I sat up slowly, pushing myself upright with arms trembling slightly. My voice barely above whispers. *"I'm not able to sleep."*

Rivaan pushed off from the doorway, entering my room quietly. *"Why?"* he asked, concerned etched on his face.

My eyes clouded, paint evident- *"I am suffering from the worst pain I have ever experienced."* Rivaan's expression softened further, he sat beside me on the bed. Gentle fingers caressing against my arms before asking- *"May I check your bandages ?"* I slowly nodded- *"Sure."*

Rivaan carefully began to undo the buttons of my nightgown sleeve. Exposing bandages, forearm and elbow, his touch sending gentle shivers. He then removed the blanket, to check the bandage on my leg injury. Blood was oozing from my leg injury. I winced slightly as he inspected the wound, his eyes narrowing. *"This need redressing. Some stitches might have torn open again."*

His fingers traced gently around the bandages, assessing damage. My eyes locked onto his profile, pain momentarily forgotten. Watching him care for my wounds with such tenderness. Rivaan swiftly changed the bandage on my leg. Applying gentle pressure to clean and dress the wound. His hands moved with precision, concern etched on his face. Once finished, he looked up at me. *"Still hurting?"* I nodded slightly, voice low. *"Ofcourse."* Rivaan's expression turned sympathetic. *"Now, I can't give you more sleeping pills or painkillers...you've already had a strong dose."* I acknowledged weakly, "Yeah."

Rivaan's gaze locked onto mine filled with compassion. He reached out gently, brushing hair behind my ear. *"Let me put you to sleep, then. No pills needed...just trust."* His voice was low, soothing. My eyelids fluttered, curiosity mixed with exhaustion. I searched his face, wondering what he meant, yet somehow trusting him completely. Rivaan wrapped his arms gently yet firmly around me, pulling me close as he whispered softly. *"My arms will do what your sleeping pills couldn't. "*

My eyelids grew heavy, breathing slowed. I nestled deeper into his embrace, feeling safe and protected. His chest rose and fell beneath her cheek, a soothing rhythm. Minutes passed like magic. My tension melted away. My pain fogged mind cleared slightly, replaced by warm comfort.

Yes, he was right. His arms indeed, did what my sleeping pills couldn't. I fell asleep in his embrace, my own cozy sanctuary found. Rivaan helped perfectly still, cherishing gentle rise and fall of my chest against his, my slow breaths a lullaby. A soft smile spread across his face, witnessing my surrender. To sleep, to trust, and perhaps...to him. He remained motionless, guarding my slumber. As moonlight continued casting its gentle glow.

Days passed swiftly. My wounds healing visibly faster. Thanks to Rivaan's devoted care and gentle affection. Zara's daily visits brought updates on Eves and our empire.

One morning, Rivaan stood by my bedside, dressing for departure. *"I have work outside city limits today. Might return very late tonight...or even tomorrow morning."* He glanced at me, expecting acknowledgment or concern for his long absence. Instead, my eyes locked onto his, sparkling softly. *"I'll wait for you."* Rivaan's expression froze. Words caught in his throat. I guess he just wasn't expecting this. He searched my gaze, sensing underlying emotion. A promise, a vow, or something more ?

Time suspended as we stared at each other. Rivaan's chest rose with a silent breath before he turned abruptly. Leaving me with only a gentle "*...take care.*" Whispered behind him. The door softly closed, I smiled faintly, already counting down moments till his return. Hours passed, Rivaan had come back around 2:00 at night. He entered my room quietly, expecting sleep. Instead, he found me sitting upright on bed, waiting for him. My eyes fixed outside, lost in thoughts, until his presence drew them back. A gentle smile spread across my face as our gazes met. Rivaan, approaching me. He said wearily- "*I'm so tired.*"

Without another word, Rivaan sat beside me, he slid slightly. Resting his head on my lap, surrendering to exhaustion. My hands instinctively cradled his head, gentle fingers threading through his hair. *"I have to follow this schedule for the coming few days..."* Rivaan trailed off. Already relaxing into my touch. I listened attentively, soothing strokes continuing through his hair. Rivaan's eyes drifted closed. I caress slowed, turning into gentle scalp massages. Lulling him towards sleep as I whispered softly. *"And I'll wait for you...every night."*

Rivaan's eyes remained closed, a soft sigh escaping his lips. His head relaxed deeper into my lap. The gentle whisper seemed to seal his fate, he was asleep instantly. I smiled softly, watching him surrender to exhaustion. My fingers continued gentle strokes through his hair, a soothing melody. As I sat there, cradling his head, feeling swirled inside me. Protective, caring...and something more profound. In this quiet moment, I realised my heart beat faster. Not just from caring for Rivaan's weary soul, but from longing for his own heart. The room faded into silence, leaving only gentle touches. Days blended together. Rivaan leaving early, returning late. I waited patiently, comforting him silently each night. No questions asked, just gentle acceptance.

One night, as he came and rested his head on my lap again, he asked me. "*Ad, I wanna know...how this La Regina Della became the La Regina Della.*"

My gaze drifted off, memorising flooding back. My voice low, haunted. "*I was never really the La Regina Della...my mother was*" I paused, collecting courage to unveil the past. "*My parents,- ma, The La Regina Della and papa, a successful businessman and a mafia, married in power.*" My eyes clouded revealing the nightmare. "*I was 18 when...when I lost my parents, my innocence...*" My voice cracked "*They killed my parents in front of me. Poured boiling oil on my parents...until they stopped screaming and died. I was helpless, held back by their men. Krish was there, hiding behind a crate...eyes wide with terror. He saw everything. Our gazes met, his silent please for help still haunts me. Something snapped...I used Ma's taught fighting skills...took down those five monsters. Killed them with my bare hands.*" My chest heaved, memories still raw. Rivaan sat back, slid closer, gentle fingers brushing hers. "*That day forget La Regina Della's legend, but also my Adira's unending pain.*" I nodded slowly, tears welling up. "*You see me, Rivaan, truly see me, for the first time anyone ever has...after Zara and of course Krish.*" Then Rivaan pacified me, and hugged me.

Next morning, everything was again normal...and then the same schedule. Rivaan again came late. And rested his head on my lap again. My fingers resumed their soothing rhythm through his hair. Suddenly my voice broke the calm atmosphere. *"Every night, whenever you're tired, sad, broken or anything else, you come to me..."* my tone turned playful yet probing. A low, throat chuckle accompanied my words. *"Who do you think I am ? Your mistress ?"*

*"My home."* His voice low, serious and devastatingly heartfelt. My fingers froze mid stroke, my breath caught. Eyes wide, searching Rivaan's face for any hint of jest. But his expression remained solemn, vulnerable. As if he'd exposed his very soul.

Time suspended. My mind reels. I hadn't anticipated this response. The gentle comforter had become the comforter, and he'd just rewritten everything. And that was the last day of the schedule. Months healed my physical wounds. My face now smooth, unblemished skin. Emotionally, I'd found solace in Rivaan's love, our bonds strengthened daily.

# CHAPTER 18
## The La Regina Della

One morning, Rivaan approached me with a hint of mischief in his eyes. *"Want to come with me on a drive...just us, nowhere specific, everywhere beautiful!"* My heart skipped beats, excitement sparkled instantly. I nodded enthusiastically, already imagining scenic routes and quality time. *"Yes."* My voice barely contained the thrill. Rushing to get ready. *"Don't lose your spark. Wear something as you usually do."* Rivaan said.

After getting ready, I felt beautiful, carefree, grabbed sunglasses, anticipating varying scenery. Turned to find Rivaan leaning against the doorway, watching me with administration. *"Stunning."* He whispered, offering his hand, my heart fluttered accepting it.

Together we walked out and sat in his Rolls-Royce Dawn convertible. The roof of the car was already open. With the car humming, we journeyed into the wild, and then, for no apparent reason, Rivaan slammed the car into park, engine purring softly. The sudden stop contrasted with the gentle wind and music. Then suddenly while on our way. My curiosity spiked as Rivaan suddenly pulled over. He killed the engine, turned to me. *"You remember I told you about a surprise for you ?"*

*"Uh-ha !"*

Rivaan stepped out of the car, gesturing to me to follow. I slid out, eyes fixed on him as he walked towards the front of the car. *"Open the truck.'* He said softly keys jungling in his hand. He pressed 'RR' button on his car keys.

My eyes widened as I peered into the trunk. I was surprised at that time. Lennox, my arch-nemesis and former ally-turned enemy, tied up in Rivaan's car trunk.

Mouth sealed with duct tape, eyes blazing with hatred and fear. I came running back to Rivaan and hugged him tightly. My arms wrapped tightly around Rivaan's neck. A fierce hug filled with emotion, gratitude, and love. Rivaan's embrace reciprocated strongly, holding me close.

Then, he gently pulled back, eyes sparkling with surprise. His hand dipped into his pocket, producing a small velvet box. My curiosity piqued as he opened it, revealing a stunning ring made with the hope diamond. 'QUEEN' engraved elegantly on the band, her heart skipped beats.

"*Queen ? Is this how you're gonna propose to me?*"

"*Nah. Not yet. My proposal to you will be history...Right now, it's just a gift for you.*"

And before I could respond, Rivaan added, "*Make a wish.*" I closed my eyes, heart overflowing one desire surface. "*I wish...to see Krish.*" Rivaan's expression turned solemn, no promise, just a gentle nod, "*Wish granted, mam.*" We shared a poignant glance before Rivaan slid the ring onto my finger. A perfect fit. Symbolic of our bond. They returned to the car. Lennox still secured in the trunk. Rivaan closed the trunk.

Rivaan started the engine, I was admiring my ring and then I asked- "*Why Queen ? I mean I've seen people giving their girls the title of princess, but never queen.*"

"*You're not my girl...you're my woman. You rule me, Adira, my world, my empire, my kingdom and my life belongs to you. You won't every piece of me as well as I do. My world and I...am nothing...without you.*"

I looked at him and smiled, I was feeling that I was the luckiest in the world. I leaned back into my seat, eyes fixed on Rivaan's profile. His jaw clenched slightly as he navigated roads with precision.

Suddenly, he turned on to a hidden driveway, trees parted like curtains revealing a 10 floor building. Rivaan stop the engine at a little distance to the building. I noticed that there were Eves and Rivaan's men scattered there. Rivaan and I stepped out. My eyes scanned the surroundings. While Rivaan leaned against his car.

Eves & Rivaan's loyal guard, stood foremost, expressionless face familial. Their usual disciplined posture remained, but eyes lacked usual spark. Faces resembled stone, no emotion, no curiosity, only dull waiting.

I sensed foreboding, something heavy weighed on their collective silence. Rivaan gestured to me, to explore further. But I was confused. As I came closer to one Eve, Eve's gaze locked into mine, still expressionless. The eve gestured me to step inside the building. And I continued walking toward the door of the building.

My heart raised as I stepped inside the abandoned building. Tension gripped my body, senses heightened for any sign of danger. But instead of threats, a familiar figure slumped against a wall caught my eye.

Krish. Alive. Yet badly Bruised, relief and anguish collided. I sprinted towards him, tears already streaming down my face. *"Krish, my little baby."* My voice cracked. A weak, beloved smile spread across Krish's face. I threw my arms around him pulling him close. Krish mirrored my embrace, wrapping arms tightly around my waist. Together we held on, tears mingling as we sobbed softly. Relief, joy and fear of almost losing each other poured out. Our emotional reunion continued uninterrupted. Until I finally pulled back slightly, eyes searching Krish's face. *"I'm sorry, I let this happen."*

*"That wasn't your fault."* Krish winced in pain, glancing past me towards the entrance. Then I and Krish came out of the building. Rivaan still leaned against his car's front. Pockets filled with hands, with a gentle smile on his face.

Krish's eyes locked into Rivaan's, I followed his gaze, and told Krish softly, *"He's the one...who saved me and found you."* Krish's expression transformed from curiosity to gratitude. He worked towards Rivaan, arms opening for an embrace. Rivaan stood tall, surprised by the gesture, yet hugged him back.

*"Thank you so much."*

*"Don't thank me, it was my duty, my right, and my responsibility."*

I smiled, witnessing their heartfelt moment. The three shared a sense of leave and new found Bond. As we prepared to leave, Rivaan's phone vibrated. His hand reached into his pocket for his phone. Unlocked it briefly. I glanced at his phone, unintentionally. A message flashed on screen- *"Sir, Lennox is missing."* My heart skipped a beat. I knew Lennox was actually in the trunk. I maintained a neutral expression, hiding my knowledge. Rivaan's eyes narrowed slightly before he switched off his phone. Pocketed it without reacting outwardly, unaware I saw the message.

*"Shall we?"* Rivaan suggested calmly before opening the car's door for us. I and Rivaan exchange a glance

before entering the vehicle. Lennox's pleasures in the trunk remained a secret for Krish. As Rivaan started the engine, I glanced at Rivaan, with a smile filled with a hint of confusion and a bit of unbelievability. Rivaan caught my smile, but it was clear that he didn't understand the reason behind it. I looked away, still smiling faintly to myself.

The car wound its way back to Rivaan's estate.

*"Where are we going now ?"*

*"Back to our mansion."*

*"No, please drop me back to my house."*

*"What ?! Is anything wrong?"*

*"No. Nothing like that, it's just, I don't wanna be a burden on you."*

*"No, tell me. Did I do something wrong?"*

*"No, Rivaan. You did nothing wrong. You remember I told you I would leave when I'll be better? I can't leave Nova Spire, like this. And I'm all better now, and I think I can take care of Krish and my empire."*

Rivaan didn't reply further. The silence comfortable among us. I glanced at Krish, still bruises but smiling weakly at the backseat. My mind still racing, thoughts swirling like a vortex. Dozens of questions collided. *"Who messaged Rivaan ? Why reveal Lennox missing ? What connects Lennox to Rivaan ? What if he is the...No, no impossible. I'm just overthinking. But what if he's the mastermind behind everything."*

My eyes locked onto Rivaan's, searching for any hint of deception. But his gaze reminded calm, inquiring only about my smile that I gave him when he caught me looking at him. My heart pounded faster, thoughts threatening to spill out. Suddenly, my expression smoothed, a Mask of calmness. *"Just happy to see Krish safe."* I said lightly, tone neutral. Avoiding my real questions, diverting attention from my true thoughts.

Finally, we arrived at our mansion. Guards and staff awaited our return. One by one, staff and guards departed. Eve lingering briefly to bow at me and Rivaan. *"Welcome back. We're relieved Krish is safe."* they said. Then Krish spoke up, exhaustion creeping into his voice. *"I need painkillers and some rest."*

I nodded, Krish headed toward his room. Leaving me and Rivaan alone in the Hall. Tension between us palpable. *"Care to explain what that smile was in the car*

? And what happened, why don't you wanna come to our mansion."

"That was nothing. And as for staying at your Mansion, I guess I had mentioned in our talks that I will leave as soon as I'll be able to walk properly, I'll be better."

"Okay, then."

"But why is Krish still bruised ? I mean for these many months you kept him in that building, without giving first aid ?"

"Actually, Ad. I lied. Lennox told me this morning about Krish's location. So, I immediately sent our people to Krish until we reach there."

"Oh. So, I have many questions."

"And I'm free to answer all of them."

"How did you find me ?"

"I black mailed the government and they asked Lennox to hand you over me, or otherwise, they would find him the culprit for the destruction of Moscow."

"So...are we going to kill Lennos or not ?"

"No, actually we can't. The government has put a ceasefire to save him."

*"Why?"*

*"Because, I later demanded for Lennox himself, the government asked him to surrender and promised him that he would be alive, so to assure him, they put a ceasefire. But it won't last long. Or if it, then we'll take Lennox somewhere else and then we can kill him."*

*"Genius."*

*"Anything else mam."*

*"Nah, I don't think so."*

# CHAPTER 19
## The La Regina Della

A few days drifted by, each one a gentle exhale after the storm. I found myself in the embrace of tranquility in the lowest living room of my mansion, my sanctuary. The soft glow of the afternoon sun filtered through the sheer curtains, painting delicate patterns on the polished marble floor. Zara sat to my left, her presence a comforting weight, her fingers lightly tracing patterns on the armrest of the plush velvet sofa. To my right, Krish leaned back, a serene smile playing on his lips as he occasionally tapped his foot in time with the barely-there melody that filled the air. It was one of those rare moments where the world outside seemed to hold its breath, allowing a pocket of perfect peace to bloom around us.

The music, a low and soothing instrumental piece, wove its way through the quiet, a gentle hum that seemed to vibrate in harmony with the stillness in my own heart. I had been lost in the comfortable silence, the kind that speaks volumes without uttering a single word, when the sudden shrill of my phone sliced through the calm. It was a jarring intrusion, yet somehow, it didn't shatter the fragile bubble completely.

With a soft sigh, I reached for the device resting on the small antique table beside me. The caller ID flashed Rivaan's name, a familiar script that always managed to stir a complex mix of emotions within me. A flicker of anticipation, a hint of apprehension – a dance I had become accustomed to.

I pressed the answer button, bringing the phone to my ear. "*Hello?*" My voice was calm, even, betraying none of the subtle shifts in my inner landscape.

And then I heard it – Rivaan's voice, deep and resonant, instantly recognizable, a familiar timbre that echoed in the quiet room. It was a sound that had once been the soundtrack to a significant chapter of my life, and even now, after everything, it still held a certain undeniable pull. His first words, whatever they might be, hung in the air, waiting to reshape the peaceful afternoon.

*"Hey, Ad. Need to head out for a work trip, just overnight to London."* I nodded, though he couldn't see me. *"Okay, when do you leave ?"*

*"Already packed. Back tomorrow night."*

*"Take care of yourself."*

"*I will.*" Then there was silence on the both sides. Rivaan asked, "*Bye ?*"

"*Yeah, bye.*"

"*I love you, Ad.*"

We exchanged brief affectionate words before hanging up. I thought nothing of his trip, assuming business as usual.

But tomorrow night passed…No Rivaan. The next day came and there was still no sign of him. No calls, no messages, unusual for Rivaan, always connected. My curiosity turned to mild concern. I tried calling him, straight to voicemail. I texted Uncle Rauf, but no response.

The sound of Rivaan's voice, though familiar, did little to soothe the unease that had been steadily growing within me like a persistent vine. Instead, it seemed to tug at a knot of worry that had been tightening in my chest for what felt like an eternity. Almost two weeks. The words echoed in the silent corners of my mind, each syllable heavy with unspoken anxieties. Two weeks without a word, without a sign. For Rivaan, a man who commanded attention and whose presence was usually a force to be reckoned with, this silence was deafening.

My concern wasn't just a fleeting worry; it was a gnawing dread that settled deep in my bones, a cold premonition that something was terribly amiss. The days that had passed since I last saw him felt like an age, each sunrise bringing with it a fresh wave of anxiety. I had become a frequent visitor to Ravenhurst, his imposing mansion that usually hummed with a certain restless energy, now felt eerily still, almost vacant. The heavy oak doors seemed to guard secrets, and the sprawling grounds held no answers.

Driven by a desperate need for information, I had also made my way to his various offices, the sleek, modern spaces that usually bustled with activity under his sharp command. But there too, I was met with a frustrating wall of polite but vague responses. His staff, usually so efficient and forthcoming, offered only carefully crafted reassurances, their smiles not quite reaching their eyes.

What truly amplified my growing fear was the unsettling nonchalance of his gang members. The men who usually moved with a palpable tension and fierce loyalty seemed... unconcerned. They offered shrugs and muttered words about Rivaan handling business out of town, or taking a much-needed break. Their lack of alarm felt jarring, almost unnatural, and it only served to fuel my suspicion that something was being deliberately concealed.

Perhaps I was overreacting, my mind conjuring worst-case scenarios. But the intuitive part of me, the instinct that had served me well in the past, screamed that something was wrong. Terribly wrong. Rivaan was not a man to simply disappear without a trace, without a word to those closest to him. This prolonged absence, coupled with the strange indifference of his inner circle, painted a disturbing picture in my mind, a picture I desperately hoped wasn't the reality. As I held the phone to my ear, waiting for Rivaan to speak, the knot in my chest tightened further, a cold dread settling in the pit of my stomach. Whatever he was about to say, I had a sinking feeling it wouldn't quell the storm of worry raging within me.

# CHAPTER 20
## Valentine

# LONDON, CLOCK TOWER

Dim light inside the ancient clock tower, gears creaking softly. Rivaan emerged from shadows, eyes blazing with intensity. Surrounded by Rao's and Lennox himself all armed. Rivaan was unarmed, but he had Crimson Requiem. He was all dressed in black.

Lennox sneered- *"Fool. Rao's will crush you like an insect."* Raos charged, Rivaan dodged initial blows with ease. Then counterattacked with precision strikes taking down thugs swiftly. Lennox watches, horrified, as his guards fall around. My work was to protect Lennox, so I wasn't attacking. Rivaan tested the clock tower door locked from outside, trapping him. Raos remained snarled, forming a semi circle around him. Rivaan eyes them calmly, an axe appearing in his hand.

One Rao thug attempted stealth, climbing up clock gears to attack from behind glass. Rivaan spun around, axe flashing upward. The rao screamed as the axe bit deep into his chest...and glass. His back was now touching the internal glass of the clock. Rivaan repeatedly stabbed at his chest, axe tearing through glass and flesh. Six brutal blows later, the rao slid down glass, dead. The glass cracked badly.

Other Raos hesitated, fearing similar gruesome demise. Rivaan advanced, axe still dripping, his eyes burning with fierce intent. *"You all...die here. Today."* Raos charged, desperate, but Rivaan wielded the axe with deadly precision.

Clock tower echoed with clashes, screams and shattering glass. Rivaan fought relentlessly, ensuring no Rao left to betray his return. Lennox sprinted wildly around the clock tower, desperate to escape Rivaan's axe. He shoved his own me forward, using them as shields against Rivaan's attacks.

*"Protect me!"* Lennox screamed, but his men filled one by one. Rivaan carved through them with a deadly precision axe biting deep into flesh. Lennox dodged barely in time, but Rivaan's axe grazed his neck horizontally. It was not a deep cut. Lennox stumbled back, eyes wide with terror. Lennox frantically pounded on the clock tower door. His fists bloody from punching metal voice hoarse from screaming.

Suddenly, he kicked the door wildly but nothing happened. Rivaan emerged from shadows axe glinting in the dim light. Lennox sensed presence and turned head slightly too late. Rivaan swung the axe downwards. But deep into Lennox's leg just above the knee. Bone cracked flesh tore, lennox screamed.

His leg severed partially barely attached. Lennox collapsed weightless leg twitching wildly. He grabbed stump agony etched on face. Rivaan stood tall axe still clutched chest heaving slowly. Rivaan kicked his partially severed leg fully detaching it. Lennox begging and screaming in pain. Lennox lay prone, chest facing floor. Rivaan sat partially on his back, weight applying pressure. Ace thrown aside clattering loudly on floor. Rivaan grasped Lennox's hair long strands wrapped around fingers. He pulled violently attempting head from torso. Lennox's body arched mouth open in silent scream. Suddenly audible, Lennox shrieked in agony, "*Ahhhhhh..!*"

Rivaan realeased hair, Lennox's head thunder back onto the floor. Rivaan inserted hai index and middle fingers of both hands into Lennox's neck wound (*the horizontal cut*) blood gushed out around fingers.

Lennox's screams grew louder, body twitching wildly. Rivaan added ring fingers, then pinkies, all fingers sinking deeper. Blood flowed faster pooling around Lennox's head. Rivaan's grip tightened fingers, digging into neck tissue.

With sudden savage strength, Rivaan ripped upwards, Lennox's head separated from body, veins dangling like macabre strings. Blood sprayed everywhere. Clock tower walls slick with crimson. Lennox's head hung from Rivaan's grasp face frozen in eternal scream. Rivaan stood, chest heaving, eyes blazing with fierce intensity. He dropped Lennox's head, it bounced once, then lay still. I was laying there pretending to be a dead body, I slightly opened up my eyes to see.

Rivaan leaned against the clock tower machinery worn stone cool against his back. He leaned his head back on the machinery, eyes closed, he breathed deeply, momentary peace amidst Carnage.

Flicked open a lighter, ignited a cigarette smoke curled lazily upwards. His gaze followed the smoke as he opened his phone, screen lit up. His jaw clenched slightly, *8067 missed calls from Adira* he stared back at the screen. He ignored them entirely, he was focused on his words. He showed no surprise or concern. Instead, he dialed a number, familiar, yet not saved in contacts. I could tell it, by the way he was sailing his number. Ringing ended quickly, low voice answered on first ring. Rivaan spoke calmly.

*"I've read your message. Lennox was stupid...of course, anybody could kidnap him."*

*Pause. Listening to the response.*

*"Don't worry. We don't care if Lennox dies."*

*Another pause. Voice on the phone is likely protesting. Rivaan then cut them off.*

*"Yeah...I wasn't able to reply because...(scratches his forehead with thumb) Adira was next to me."*

*Final instructions*

*"Don't call me from now onwards."*

Phone slid shut, the call ended abruptly. Rivaan took another drag. Eyes narrowing slightly. Secrets upon secrets, Adira remained oblivious nearby. He exhaled smoke slowly contemplating next moves. Rivaan stood frozen, cigarette smoke curling around his face.

Bloodstained clothes clung to his body. Lennox's life force still drying on fabric.

He took another slow drag, eyes fixed on nothing, yet absorbing everything. Rivaan's gaze wandered, phone still clutched in bloody hand. He switched it off again, plunging himself into temporary darkness from Adira's reach. Then, his eyes drifted upward, through grimy clock tower windows. Transfixed by outer beauty, warm orange sunset hues danced across the sky. Soft pink and purple tones bleeding into the horizon, peacefulness mocked bloodshed below. Rivaan's chest rose and fell slowly, cigarette smoke escaped lips. He seemed mesmerized by sunset serenity, fleeting escape from carnage and secrets. His bloody reflection stared back from window glass juxtaposed with dying light. A haunting silhouette. Rivaan, forever bound to shadows and darkness.

Rivaan then again switched on his phone, and dialed to his man, who might be standing outside the clock tower machinery room's door. Rivaan's voice low and commanding through the phone. *"Open the door, now."*

Clock tower doors cracked open. Rivaan before stepping out said, *"No need to hide, I'm done killing."* I realised that he was saying to me. I stood up, and watched him leave. Rivaan stepped out, an imposing figure emerging from the shadows. His men fell into formation around him, immediately escorting him. All exceed 6 feet tall- bulky frames clad entirely in black. Rivaan towered among them, a dangerous aura palpable. Face smeared with blood, eyes narrowing as he scanned the surroundings. Vertical torso visible through half open black shirt. Chiseled abdomen and chest visible, black coat draped open over shoulder. Cigarette dangling from fingers, smoke curling lazily upwards. Hazardous gaze swept the area, daring anyone to approach. Rivaan excluded unbridled power, unstoppable force. His men moved synchronously, silent guardians, eyes fixed outward, warning potential threats to keep distance.

Group moved forward, an ominous procession cutting through crowds. People parted instinctively. His reputation precedes, fear trailed behind like shadow.

# CHAPTER 21
## The La Regina Della

Me, Zara, and Krish, we all were sitting in the living room of our mansion. Living room field with concern. I pacing slowly, eyes sunken from sleepless nights. Zara and Krish seated on the sofa, exchanging worried glances. While I was standing, facing inside, my back facing the Opened entrance door of our mansion. Zara spoke up. *"Is it necessary that everyone has to get kidnapped one by one?"*

*"Bullshit. I don't believe it. He cannot get kidnapped...but he might kidnap."* I said. Then my gaze drifted off, lost again in thoughts of Rivaan's disappearance. Suddenly a deep voice boomed from the garden of my mansion. *"QUEEN...!"*

My heart skipped a beat, a familiar tone sent shivers down my spine. I spun around, eyes locking onto the speaker. Time froze, my mind barely processing what I saw. Rivaan stood in the garden, an imposing figure dominating the space.

My eyes locked onto his, confirmation sparkling within. No doubt remained, the voice, the presence, the piercing gaze. ALL RIVAAN.

My heart raced wildly, emotions swirling like a storm. Relief, shock, anger, love, tangled mess inside my chest. His pleasures commanded attention, voice still resonating.

"*Queen...*" he whispered softer now. My breath caught, I felt like I'd need punched in the chest. Zara and Krish rose slowly. But I remained froze, drinking in Rivaan's presence. He was all clean, with white shirt and blue jeans, giving him an elegant look. My focus fixed on his eyes, searching for answers to countless questions.

"*Rivaan...*" I barely whispered, voice trembling slightly. I took a step forward, then froze, unsure what to do next. Rivaan stood still, watching my reaction, awaiting my move. The room behind me melted away, only Rivaan existed.

Zara and Krish, silent spectators to this reunion. My voice barely above whispers, lips forming a single word. "*Rivaan...*" Waiting for him to speak, to explain, to breathe again. Rivaan had a black mini suitcase in his hand.

My restraint shattered, I sprinted towards Rivaan. Arms open wide, embracing him fiercely. My head buried in his chest, tears streaming down face. Rivaan's eyes closed, his arms wrapping tightly around me. Holding me close, cheek pressed against me, below ear.

Together we stood, frozen in emotional reunion. Tears soaked Rivaan's white shirt, my sobbing muffled against him. His hands gently stroked my back, a comforting gesture. The place around us melted away, only heart beats remained. I pulled back slightly, tears drying slowly, eyes searching Rivaan's face. *"Where were you ? Why didn't..."* Rivaan's finger gently pressed against my lips. *"Shhh queen...no questions...yet."* He smiled softly, eyes filled with affection. *"You look stunning, even tears stained. Beauty marks suit you."*

My cheeks flushed, Rivaan's compliment distracting me momentarily. He continued praising. *"Your hair, still perfectly set. Your skin, glowing like moonlight. And your eyes...still holding my soul captive...miss you more than words can express."*

Rivaan sank down onto his knees, graceful movement despite suit. I stood before him, surprised by the sudden gesture. He grasped both my hands gently, thumbs stroking my skin. Eyes locking intensely upward, burning with emotion. My heart skipped beats, mesmerized by Rivaan's kneeling form. His light brown hair perfectly messy, and in the sunlight he looked at me with love. His son kissed face, expressing nervousness. In the sunlight he looked even more handsome, then he ever could. Devotion etched on his face, his thumbs continued gentle caress, hands cradling mine. He started,

*"From the moment I met you, my queen. You became my reason, for breathing, for ruling, for living. Together we'll rule our Empire, your every waking thoughts. Every breath, every decision, forever entwined with your existence. Adira...from chaos, you emerged, my salvation, my queen. Together we'll dance in darkness, our love a twisted, beautiful hell. I want eternity with you, officially, forever...my wife. My forever Queen to rule beside me, over my heart and our kingdom. You belong to me, Adira...in every shadow of your soul. Adira...you're my one and only desire. Will you marry me ? And I'll claim every breath, every heartbeat...every nightmare of yours. Say yes...and I'll worship you, obsessively, violently, forever. Refuse...and I'll still make you mine, by any means necessary."*

Rivaan then gently freed both hands, reaching them to the suitcase. Picked up the suitcase, and started opening it. Rivaan's gesture mimicked opening a ring box, but sinister intent lurked. He lifted the suitcase lid slowly, revealing eerie darkness within. Lennox's severed head stared back, dead eyes frozen in terror. Rivaan's gaze never left mine. When I saw Lennox's head, I was over the moon, I was the happiest. That's when I realised how obsessed he was. His dark triad traits made him irresistible—his confidence was alluring, his cunning was thrilling, and his lack of remorse only made me crave his attention more. He wasn't just charming—he was dangerously intoxicating, his words a trap—crafted by a high-IQ narcissist with an unshakable ego, with the cold precision of a psychopath who knew exactly how to make me crave him. I was just another victim of his brilliance. Rivaan continued. *"Will you be my queen in...darkness ?"*

For a fleeting second, I hesitated—but then, with a quiet surrender, I accepted his proposal and sealed my fate as his wife. for I nodded slowly, tears streaming down my face, whispering Barely audible. *"Yes...forever yours."*

Rivaan's face lit up with triumphant passion. He slammed the suitcase shut. Lennox's head hidden from view once more. He then rose swiftly, towering over me, before gently pulling me close. And he kissed me, fierce, possessive kiss consuming is both.

I melted into his arms, my arms wrapping tightly around his neck, sealing my fate as his forever. The suitcase with Lennox's head lay forgotten, of

Rivaan's obsession. Now overshadowed by Rivaan's obsession with me. He broke the kiss, lips brushing my ears. "*My queen...mine forever.*"

I smiled, lost in his darkness, whispering back. "*Forever yours...my kind.*"

# CHAPTER 22
## Zara

Krish and I stood frozen just inside the doorway, our eyes glued to Adira and Rivaan. The scene we had just witnessed in the study, the cold, calculated exchange with Finnick, the casual acceptance of morally gray actions – it left a knot of unease in my stomach.

*"He is a devil, but he did it for my sister,"* Krish murmured, his voice barely above a whisper, a strange mix of resentment and reluctant understanding in his tone.

"*Yeah,*" I replied softly, my gaze still fixed on Adira's profile. There was a new hardness to her, a sharper edge that seemed to have been honed by her interactions with Rivaan.

*"But how can someone be so cruel?"* Krish's voice was filled with a genuine bewilderment, a lingering innocence that I sometimes envied.

I sighed, my gaze shifting to him. "*Have you ever really seen your sister, Krish? They both are the same, even we all are, in our own ways.*" The darkness wasn't just outside of us; it resided within, a potential we all possessed.

Krish was quiet for a moment, his brow furrowed in thought. "*You know I always used to think...that he likes my sister. But now I am convinced...he is obsessed over her."* There was a note of worry in his voice, a fear for Adira's autonomy in the face of Rivaan's intense focus.

*"Krish, do you think they'll actually...gonna marry, happily?"* I asked, the word "happily" feeling almost foreign in the context of everything we had just witnessed.

He glanced towards the study, a dark humor flickering in his eyes. *"After what we just witnessed, suitcase gate with Lennox's head, yeah...likely."* The casual brutality of it still sent a shiver down my spine.

A wave of sadness washed over me. *"Adira's going far, far away from us. We are losing her."* It wasn't just a physical distance; it was an emotional one, a growing chasm carved out by her choices and her entanglement with Rivaan.

*"She'll disappear into his Empire,"* Krish added, his voice heavy with resignation.

*"We'll just have formal visits from now,"* I said, the thought feeling cold and sterile. The easy camaraderie we once shared felt like a distant memory.

We both shared worried glances, a silent acknowledgment of the shift in our family dynamic. Then Krish added, a flicker of hope in his eyes, *"But I don't think so. She loves us both more than him, she won't disappear."* He was trying to convince himself as much as me.

*"I'll convince it to myself,"* I echoed, the words feeling hollow.

*"But she got a nice husband, with a nice future, and a nice family...and so nice, nice babies,"* Krish continued, the forced cheerfulness in his voice not quite reaching his eyes.

A small smile touched my lips despite the underlying worry. *"I'll build my home, next to them."* The thought of staying close, of maintaining some semblance of connection, offered a sliver of comfort.

Just then, Adira and Rivaan turned and started walking towards us. As they approached, my gaze involuntarily flickered to the suitcase, a wave of disgust washing over me. *"I hope Lennox goes to heaven,"* I blurted out, the words laced with a dark sarcasm.

"*Why?*" Rivaan asked, his golden eyes narrowing slightly, a hint of amusement playing on his lips.

"*Cause you'll be ruling hell... just kidding, we'll be in hell, after all that we did,*" I replied, a nervous laugh escaping my lips. The absurdity of our situation, the casual acceptance of violence and morally questionable actions, was almost comical in a twisted way.

And surprisingly, a genuine laugh bubbled up from Adira, followed by a low chuckle from Rivaan. For a brief moment, the tension eased, the shared darkness a strange kind of bond. We continued walking deeper into the mansion, the weight of our actions and the uncertain future still lingering, but for now, the shared laughter offered a temporary reprieve.

# La Regina Della

## As Narrator

I then took a glance at Rivaan's smiling face. I was happy but somewhere in the back of my mind, the question still roamed free. *Who is the mastermind? Why did Rivaan send me to Moscow to bring that suitcase ? What was there in the suitcase ? Where Rivaan used to go when I was injured ? Who messaged Rivaan that day ? And why informed him Lennox is missing ? What connects Rivaan to Lennox ? What if it was all planned ? Just a trap ? Is it all finished ? Or was it just a beginning or a teaser ? What if the mastermind is someone...I know...I trust...I love ?*

# To be continued...

# ABOUT THE BOOK

Step into the treacherous world of Rostov-on-Don, where the seductive allure of power clashes with the brutal realities of organized crime. Adira, the formidable and enigmatic leader known as 'The La Regina Della,' finds her carefully constructed empire threatened when her brother is taken.

Her relentless pursuit of his kidnappers plunges her into a dangerous game of alliances and betrayals, forcing her to confront rival mafias and make morally ambiguous choices. In this shadowy landscape, she finds herself entangled with Rivaan, a powerful and equally ruthless figure, their connection a volatile mix of dark attraction and strategic maneuvering.

As Adira navigates the deadly intricacies of the Russian underworld, the lines between right and wrong blur, and the cost of power becomes increasingly steep. From tense negotiations to explosive confrontations, 'The Devil Head' delves into the depths of human ambition, obsession, and the lengths one will go to protect what they claim as their own.

# ABOUT THE AUTHOR

Syren Ravenwood is a thirteen-year-old author with a vivid imagination and a penchant for exploring the darker facets of human nature. "The Devil Head" is her debut novel, a thrilling dive into the gritty world of organized crime, penned with a maturity and intensity that belies her young age.

From a young age, Syren found herself drawn to complex characters and intricate narratives. With the unwavering support of her mother and her side of the family, she nurtured her passion for storytelling, weaving tales that often surprised and captivated those around her. Her best friend has also been a constant source of encouragement, fueling her creative fire.

"The Devil Head" marks Syren's first foray into the world of published fiction. Through her writing, she delves into themes of power, loyalty, and the blurred lines between good and evil, crafting a narrative that is sure to grip readers and leave a lasting impression. Syren Ravenwood is a fresh and bold voice in the literary landscape, and "The Devil Head" is just the beginning of what promises to be a compelling writing journey.

www.ingramcontent.com/pod-product-compliance
Lightning Source LLC
LaVergne TN
LVHW041703070526
838199LV00045B/1181